A VALLEY CALLED CANAAN

1885 - 2002

Edwin Daryl Michael

Illustrated with sketches
by Kenneth Kreider

MCCLAIN PRINTING COMPANY
Parsons, West Virginia

International Standard Book Number 0-87012-684-9
Library of Congress Catalog Card Number 2002110750
Printed in the United States of America

Camera-ready material provided.

McClain Printing Company
Parsons, West Virginia 26287
www.mcclainprinting.com
2002

CONTENTS

DEDICATION

Dedicated to Jane, whose assistance, encouragement, and support made it all possible, to my mother Isolene, who gave me a love of books, to my father, Edward Beatty Michael, who fostered my love of the outdoors, and to Ruffee, who created so many special memories.

CREDITS

Front cover photo was provided by Jim Clark and the back cover photo was provided by Mary Burnette, National Wildlife Federation.

The Canaan Valley map was prepared by Corey Anderson, with the Canaan Valley Institute.

Funding for the map, illustrations, and professional editing was provided by the Canaan Valley Institute.

ACKNOWLEDGMENTS

The author is indebted to many individuals, groups, and agencies that have made this book possible. While hundreds have contributed, the following played major roles during the thirty years that this book was in the making: Sandy and Steve Brown, Mary Burnette, Jim Clark, Bob Collins, Julie Dzaack (and Amy, Erin, and Megan), Ron Fortney, Rob Gilligan, William Goudy, Dave Harkins, Frank Jernejcic, Norm Julian, Al Kave, Ken Kreider, Homer McCarthy, Tom Pauley, Ron Preston, Jim Rawson, Robert Thomas, Scott Shalaway, Linda Smith, Kenny Sturm, Stuart Welch, David White, Paula Worden, David Young, and Pete Zurbuch.

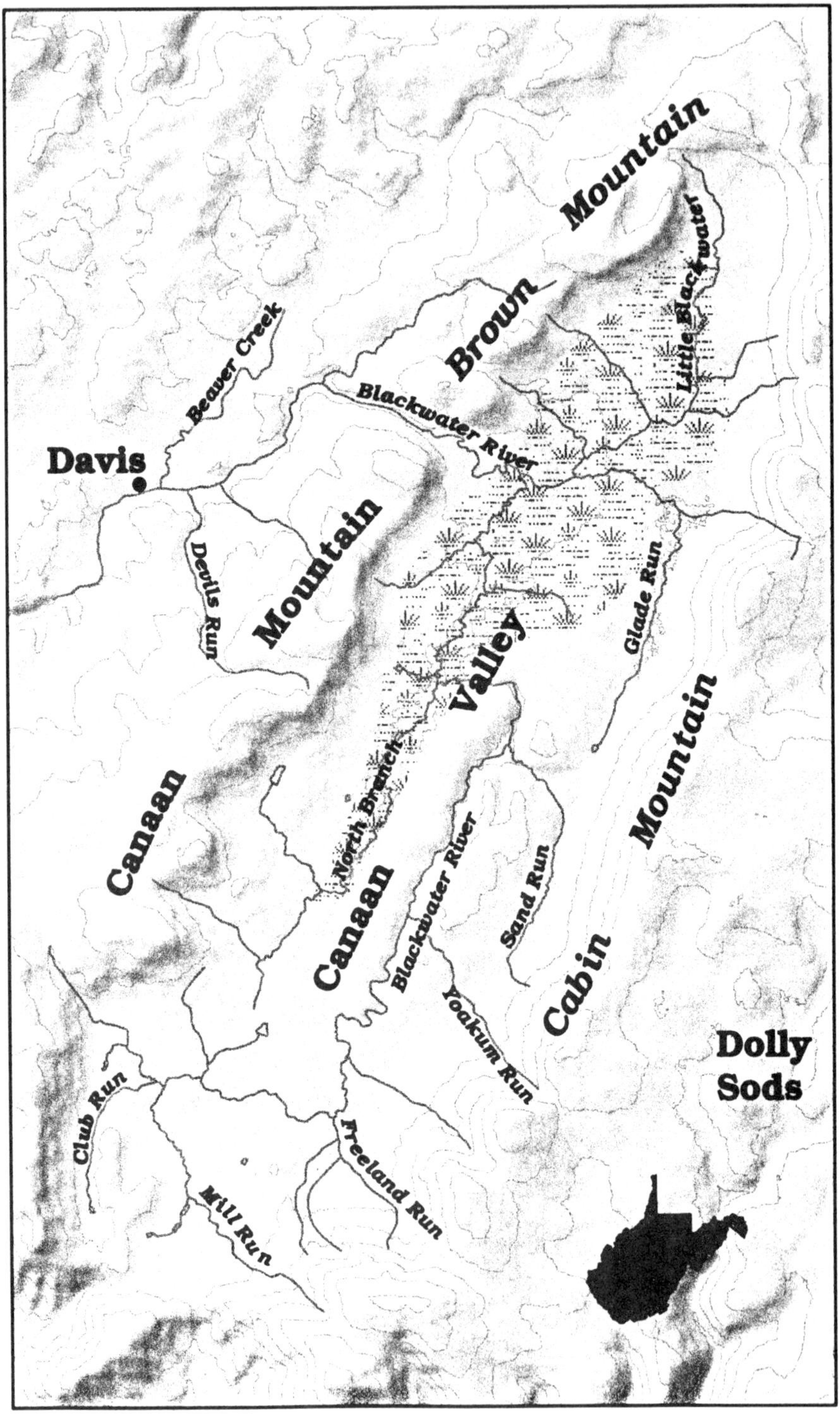
Brown Mountain
Little Blackwater
Beaver Creek
Blackwater River
Davis
Devils Run
Mountain
Valley
Glade Run
Cabin Mountain
Canaan
North Branch
Canaan
Blackwater River
Sand Run
Yoakum Run
Dolly Sods
Club Run
Freeland Run
Mill Run

PROLOGUE

Canaan Valley is a fascinating, unique, geological phenomenon, supporting an equally fascinating, unique mosaic of plant and animal communities. Spelled like the Biblical Land of Canaan, it is pronounced Kuh-na'ne, accenting the second syllable and giving it a long "a" sound.

Only a few individuals fully comprehend the changes in the Earth's surface that led to monumental upheaval and formed ancient mountains now known as the Appalachians. Fewer still can envision the millennia required for these events to occur. The tumultuous thrusting and uplifting created mountains higher, and older, than the current Rockies. Even the most resistant rocks, however, cannot withstand the forces of wind and water, freezing and thawing. Water especially, is a powerful force, and given several million years, relentless erosion shrank the mountains around Canaan Valley to a height of "only" four thousand feet.

In addition to wearing away the tops of mountains, erosion created Canaan Valley's oval-shaped basin; characterized by smooth hills and wide stream bottoms. The forty square mile, elevated basin, is surrounded by Brown, Cabin, and Canaan mountains, and is drained by the Blackwater River. This dark sluggish river falls only one hundred feet in a distance of twelve miles as it flows across the relatively flat valley floor. In contrast, after emerging from a gap between Brown and Canaan mountains, the character of the Blackwater River changes significantly. After leaving the Valley and flowing past the town of Davis, the river becomes a savage torrent as it begins a wild and tumultuous drop through the Blackwater Canyon, plunging over one thousand feet in a distance of only ten miles.

Waters from Canaan Valley follow a convoluted course that ultimately reaches the Gulf of Mexico near New Orleans. The darkly stained waters flowing from the bogs and beaver ponds in Canaan Valley join other waters from north central West Virginia, eventually merging with yet other waters from the central United States. In the course of their great journey, waters from the Valley named Canaan contribute successively to the Cheat, Monongahela, Ohio, and Mississippi rivers.

Nowhere in the United States did there exist a more luxuriant growth of spruce and hemlock than that existing in Canaan Valley when the first settlers ventured into this mountain wilderness. No saw had scarred the trees, standing so thick that sunlight never reached the damp forest floor. As land-hungry settlers pushed through the Appalachians, however, few, if any, wild areas remained untouched. While geological forces created the unique, raised anticline valley rimmed with folded mountains, humans are responsible for the surface landscape that now blankets the valley. The sphagnum bogs, beaver ponds, darkly stained waterways, exposed boulder fields, and mosaic of plant communities present a tundra-like landscape resembling a landform of the far north rather than anything in the Central Appalachians.

Compared to most other regions of the Appalachians, the recorded human history of Canaan Valley is relatively short. More than 250 years have passed since the first known visit by an explorer, and 115 years since the first commercial loggers brought their crosscut saws, double-bitted axes, and log peaveys into this valley wilderness.

The historical narrative in this book relates the actual events of the 1885-2002 era. In addition, it describes the natural history of some of the more prominent wildlife species that witnessed the apparent destruction and subsequent rebirth of this thirty-six-thousand-acre ecosystem. The bogs and the life within are priceless gifts of the Ice Age, but their future is balanced in human hands.

CHAPTER ONE

1885: WILDERNESS VALLEY

The large female snapping turtle cautiously crawled out of the slow-moving river and inched herself up the sandy bank. Darkness settled like a thick blanket over the small wilderness river that flowed through Canaan Valley, and a drizzly rain began to fall. The eight lonesome hoots of a barred owl drifted from an ancient hemlock perched at the river's edge, but the turtle had nothing to fear from this large owl or any other predatory bird. Her powerful jaws and knife-sharp claws were a match for any predator in Canaan Valley, and the soft vulnerable parts of her body were protected by her carapace—the bony shell that functioned as natural armor. Unseasonably warm, the light rain was a sharp contrast to the snow flurries and sleety rains that had pelted the river and the hemlock trees during the previous two weeks. In the mountains of West Virginia, weather during the first week of June could be quite erratic, as warm sunny days were interspersed with periods of sleet and rain.

This important journey of twenty yards to the turtle's sandy destination was triggered by the warm rain that was nearly fifteen degrees warmer than the Blackwater River. The heavy-shelled turtle was making her annual trip to the same site she had visited each June for the past twenty-six years. Moving slowly but purposefully through the deertongue grass, the bulky female finally reached her destination.

The snapping turtle, adapted for life in the river, was obviously out of her element when moving on land. The short powerful legs that carried her to the sandy spot were not adapted for land locomotion, but they were perfectly adapted for the task at hand that night. The female positioned herself in the chosen place so that she was firmly anchored by her front feet, while her hind feet commenced digging in an awkward, but effective manner. Alternating one hind foot with the other, her long claws and broad muscular feet began long sweeping scoops from side to side beneath her tail. Sand grabbed by the right hind foot was piled to the right, while sand grabbed by the left hind foot was piled to the left. As the hole deepened, the rain-moistened sand received more moisture as the female instinctively urinated into the hole. After nearly two hours, the hole reached a size where the hind legs, tail, and end of her shell were out of sight.

For the next three hours the female remained stationary, hanging on the edge of the hole. Although she appeared motionless, small, white, round eggs were being slowly and systematically deposited into the flask-shaped cavity. A white-tailed doe nearly stepped on the motionless turtle, but neither the turtle nor the doe were alarmed at the chance encounter. When the total number of eggs reached thirty-two, the female crawled forward away from her slanted perch on the edge of the hole and, with reverse scrapes, began pushing the sandy soil back in on top of her eggs. The task of making the eggs covert required nearly an hour. Rotating her body 180 degrees, the turtle faced the hole as if to assess her efforts.

She had selected a site where conditions were suitable for development of her eggs. The soil would remain damp enough to prevent desiccation but not too wet to limit exchange of air through the eggshell. No trees were present at the site, and the sun's rays would warm the soil enough to provide the incubation temperatures necessary for development of baby turtles. Apparently contented with the results, the female laboriously retreated to the safety of the river where she would spend the next twelve months before repeating the vital egg-laying behavior.

The rain stopped the next day, and after darkness had settled over the Valley the resident nocturnal animals began their activities. Spring peepers called from a shallow cove at the river's edge and a beaver gnawed on an aspen tree growing on the hillside. The unearthly notes of a saw-whet owl drifted through the trees while a raccoon moved silently along the edge of the river in search of its evening meal. Not particular about its diet, this carnivore eagerly consumed any small animal it could capture. A pickerel frog or a crayfish, a spotted salamander or even a water snake would make a welcome meal. Raccoons did not typically chase down or ambush their prey as did the fox, bobcat, and weasel; as hunters, however, they were just as proficient as other carnivores.

Unsuccessful along the river's edge, the hungry raccoon wandered up the bank and began searching for food through the tall grass. Although the rain had washed away most of the turtle odor at the nest, the ever-alert raccoon detected the faint scent of disturbed soil and the strange urine odor deposited by the female turtle. Raising its head above the wet grass to locate the interesting odor, the quivering nostrils soon targeted the source and the raccoon quickly covered the short distance to the disturbed soil that covered the thirty-two eggs.

Raccoons have the most adept front paws of any carnivore. Their long fingers enable them to obtain food that other carnivores cannot, and this raccoon soon dug down through the five inches of sandy soil to the eggs. Pulling out one of the round white eggs, the raccoon sat up on its haunches and used canine teeth to pierce the leathery shell. The yellow yolk was quickly lapped up by the raccoon's long tongue and the empty eggshell was casually dropped near the nest. Six more eggs were retrieved from the nest by the long, nimble fingers and the nutritious yolk was lapped out of the shell as quickly as possible. The raccoon, meticulous in its eating habits, smeared only a small amount of the sticky yellow yolk on its distinctive black mask.

The raccoon was not the only hungry predator hunting along the Blackwater River that night. A long-legged, tawny bobcat had detected the odor of the raccoon and cautiously stalked to within fifteen feet before stopping to crouch in the tall grass. An adult raccoon might have sensed the bobcat, but this yearling raccoon was too preoccupied with the tasty turtle eggs. The bobcat was an adult female, hunting to feed her two hungry kittens waiting in a small rock cave above the Valley floor.

As the bobcat's short tail twitched slowly, razor-sharp claws alternately extended and retracted with precision. Gathering its legs under the twenty-six pound body to gain maximum propulsion, the bobcat burst from the grass and in two bounds was on top of the nine-pound raccoon. Although the raccoon had more teeth than the bobcat, the extra teeth were premolars and molars—chewing teeth. Four of the bobcat's twenty-eight teeth, however, were long dagger-like canines designed for penetration through fur or feathers of prey. The bobcat's killing canines easily penetrated the raccoon's neck and small drops of blood seeped from the puncture wounds as the bobcat shook its prey several times to extinguish the last bit of life from the smaller carnivore.

During the short struggle between the two mammals, dirt was pushed back into the small hole where the remaining turtle eggs lay. After the kill, the bobcat urinated at the site and clawed the sandy soil with its hind legs. This scraping behavior, typical of members of the cat family, camouflaged the nest and the bobcat urine acted as a deterrent to two other raccoons passing near the turtle nest the next night. A heavy thunderstorm swept through the Valley two days later and all evidence of the turtle nest was obliterated.

With the danger of predation eliminated for the next few months, the remaining turtle eggs were unthreatened and within two months the head, tail, and legs were recognizable on the developing embryos. Nourished by the yolk within each eggshell, the embryos evolved into miniatures of their mother. Inside each of the twenty-five eggs, faint movements were occurring. While the young were not yet aware of life above ground, the vibrations of every leg twitch and every neck stretch were sensed by each small turtle within the clutch of stacked eggs.

Rainfall was below average during that summer in 1885, with only six inches of rain falling between May and September. However, sand moisture around the eggs was maintained by saturation from the water table and by the heavy fogs that blanketed the river bottom most mornings. The dense coniferous forest that enveloped the flood plain eliminated drying winds and provided the high humidity that supplemented the occasional summer rain.

The climate of Canaan Valley was similar to that of the great coniferous forests extending across Canada, and the summer of 1885 was even cooler than usual. Ground temperature averaged only sixty-nine degrees; as a result all of the embryos developed into females. Had the ground temperatures been between seventy-two and eighty degrees, all of the embryos would have developed into males. This phenomenon is characteristic of snapping turtles throughout North America and, although not totally unique, is somewhat unusual among other reptiles.

By September, the young turtles were still growing inside the slightly expanded and protective leathery eggshells. Although their eyes were closed, their shells soft, and their bones flexible, they were near full development. Winter arrived early that year, temperatures dropped into the teens on several September nights and four inches of snow fell before the first of October. Soil temperatures around the turtle eggs dropped into the low fifties and as a result further embryonic development was stopped for the year. Hatching did not occur that fall and the baby turtles spent their first winter in a state of torpor within the protective eggshells. Cold air flooded the Valley and more than 160 inches of snow fell that winter. The young turtles, however, remained safe—if not actually warm. The snow provided insulation and, fortunately for the turtles, temperatures within the nest did not drop below freezing.

By late March, spring-like weather arrived and the sandy soil along the riverbank gradually warmed above fifty degrees, triggering movements within several of the eggs. By the first week of April the movements became more regular and the eggs trembled imperceptibly. The surrounding sand absorbed these slight vibrations. So it was that raccoons, black bears, and river otter searching for food along the riverbank were unaware of the potential meal directly beneath them.

By April most of the snow and ice had melted and soil temperatures were slowly rising as the sun ascended ever higher during its arc from east to west. Meanwhile, a small sharp protuberance had developed on the nose of each turtle during the late stages of development. This "egg-tooth" served only one purpose, to slit the leathery shell and free the young turtle. Instinct guided the miniature turtles' struggles within their shells and shortly thereafter a head emerged, followed by front legs and then the entire individual. During the next six hours, nineteen of the young turtles emerged from their shells. Four of the twenty-five eggs failed to develop and two of the young turtles were unable to escape from the shell that became a death chamber.

Hatching was occurring at other nests throughout Canaan Valley and a new generation of snapping turtles was ready to enter the world. Upon emerging from their shells, the baby turtles filled their lungs with the life-giving air that had filtered through the sand. The turtles did not immediately attempt to leave the nest, but remained huddled together for the next four days. On the fifth night they instinctively began to dig upward, pushing slowly to the surface. Of the nineteen baby turtles that had hatched from their shells, only fourteen were able to emerge from the soil. The other five lacked adequate body reserves and were too weak to tunnel through the sand. Although the deaths of these baby turtles were unfortunate, this loss would have no measurable effect on the population of snapping turtles within the Canaan Valley ecosystem. As with most wildlife, a surplus of young was produced each year to allow for never-ending mortality.

Where there is life there is also death. During their first few years of life the young turtles would be subjected to constant predation, with only a few surviving to adulthood. While most of the turtles that emerged from the nest were equally fit, only fate would determine which would succumb to predation, which to weather, and which to unpredictable accidents. As they crawled out of their shells and later dug upward through the sand, the first struggles of their lives were guided by instinct, as would be most activities essential to the survival of turtles. Logic and reason play an insignificant role in the actions of snapping turtles—and most other reptiles.

The baby turtles began emerging from the soil as the first faint signs of dawn penetrated the fog that covered the river. As they adjusted to their new environment, they remained quietly at the soil surface, but they could not remain there long. Their survival depended upon reaching the safety of the Blackwater River. To a small turtle the size of a fifty-cent piece, the sixty-foot struggle through the grass was one of several tests they had to pass to enter the world of the snapping turtle. Most turtle babies are precocial at birth and receive no parental care. They are nearly fully developed at hatching and resemble an adult turtle. The mother does not assist in incubation, in emergence from the nest, or in travel to the water. She does not teach them to avoid predators and does not assist them in finding food. The mother turtle has only one responsibility, to lay the eggs that will act as the vehicle to transmit her genetic attributes to future generations of snapping turtles.

Although all fourteen of the young turtles were physically capable of reaching the river, they would not all make it. A pair of ravens was nesting in a large red spruce snag on the opposite side of the river. Spotting a slight movement in the grass, the male raven sailed across the river to investigate. Unlike turtles, most avian parents play an essential role in the survival of their offspring. One of their many responsibilities is to insure that their young receive adequate protection and nourishment. The raven's mate was sitting on three eggs and the male was constantly searching for food for the female as she incubated their future offspring. Ravens are primarily meat-eaters, consuming invertebrates, small birds, small mammals, and carrion.

The newly hatched, small turtles were easy targets for the male raven who flew down and quickly killed two of the young with sharp stabs of his beak. He carried these back to the nest where he tenderly transferred them to his mate and then quickly returned to satisfy his own hunger. Four of the small turtles had reached the water and thus escaped the sharp beak of the raven, but the others were not quite so lucky. A baby turtle is no match for a raven, or any other predator, and the raven efficiently dispatched three more of the helpless young. Their shells had not yet hardened and the male raven easily swallowed the three young and then hopped through the grass in search of more. The last of the young turtles had reached the edge of the riverbank and tumbled over when the raven made a swoop toward it. As the turtle fell into the water the raven managed to grab it by one leg. Although the baby turtle struggled, it was helpless in the beak of this coal-black predator that was so well equipped for survival.

As the raven headed toward his mate with the baby turtle, a large dark bird suddenly appeared above the tree canopy near the raven nest. Ravens have few enemies, but this bird with a seven-foot wingspan was a golden eagle, capable of killing ravens or any other large birds that resided in the coniferous forest. Fearing that the large raptor was a threat to his mate on the nest, the male raven opened his beak to direct a loud vocal warning at the eagle. Suddenly freed from certain death, the baby turtle plunged directly toward the river and the large rocks so abundant in this section of the Blackwater. Only a few seconds passed as the helpless turtle plunged toward the rocks. Fate smiled on this particular individual, however, and she landed with a small splash in the safety of the water. Thus began the life of the female turtle that one day would be the oldest living animal in Canaan Valley.

CHAPTER TWO

1886: THE BLACKWATER RIVER

Hitting the cold Blackwater River after falling nearly forty feet was a shock, but it caused no harm to the flexible little turtle. After sinking slowly to the bottom of the dark river the turtle remained motionless for several minutes. The respiratory system of the turtle had experienced two shocks during the last few days. The initial shock came when the turtle emerged from her nest and began breathing the cool fresh air that blanketed the Valley floor. The second shock came when the turtle was abruptly dropped into the Blackwater River, sinking to depths where normal breathing was impossible. Years of evolution had adapted snapping turtles to spend long periods of time underwater without the necessity of coming to the surface every few minutes to obtain atmospheric oxygen, and the hatchling was in no danger of drowning.

The little turtle instinctively swam to the surface where she pulled in the life-giving air that was so essential to all air-breathing animals. The turtle was equipped with traits to survive without parental assistance, and upon reaching the surface she immediately began paddling toward shore. Swimming, like digging and breathing and crawling, was a behavior that did not have to be learned. Although probably unaware of the many dangers facing vulnerable young animals, the small turtle seemed drawn to the protection of the shoreline. She had survived the near fatal brush with death in the beak of a raven, but would have to survive many more near-death situations if she were to reach adulthood. The Blackwater River and the associated bottomlands were home to several predators in addition to the raccoon, raven, and bobcat. The newly emerged baby turtles that managed to reach the safety of the Blackwater River had to learn quickly to avoid predators such as the mink, river otter, water snake, and great blue heron. These and other predators such as large fish and adult snapping turtles would not hesitate to catch and eat small turtles.

The threat of death was everywhere and ever present, waiting in the tall spruce trees, in the cool dark waters of the Blackwater

River, and in the sky. To survive, a young turtle had to constantly avoid the multitude of hungry predators sharing its world.

The shoreline, with its overhanging bank, provided more protection from predators than did the few rocks in the middle of the river. The roots of the occasional speckled alder and rhododendron, plus the mat of narrow-leaf pondweeds growing in shallow and slow-moving water created a safe refuge. For the next five months the river's edge was to be the home of the baby female turtles that had safely reached the river. Not all would survive; only one or two would still be alive when the first autumn snow flurries fell, signaling the time to enter hibernation.

During the next few hours of breathing, swimming, and resting, the female turtle tentatively explored the newly entered environment where she must learn to survive. As with most newborn animals, there were two immediate problems that had to be solved—finding food to eat, and escaping predation. The turtle had experienced the threat of being eaten when the raven attacked her. But she survived. The yolk sac, which was attached to her lower shell, and body reserves would nourish her for a few days but she had no mother to teach her what was edible. She had to learn what foods were safe and nutritious, and do so within the next four days or she would die of starvation.

This baby turtle had never opened its mouth to grasp food, had never had food in its mouth, and had never swallowed a bite of food. If her instincts were not strong the baby turtle would starve. First, she had to feel the urge to eat, then she had to determine how to eat. All of the baby turtles that had dug out of their nests and entered the Blackwater River that spring had to learn to eat with no assistance.

Biologists assigned the scientific name of Chelydra serpentina to the common snapping turtle. This species has the widest geographic range of any reptile in North America, extending from Canada to Florida and west to the Rocky Mountains. The genus name of Chelydra, which means water serpent, was not truly descriptive of the baby turtle at this stage in her life, but it would be quite appropriate when she reached adulthood. While her shell had hardened slightly during the few days after she emerged from her shell, it was still flexible around the edges. By the end of her first summer it would become rigid. When she was mature the shell would be hard enough to withstand the crushing claws of a black bear, the horrific pressures from a mountain lion's canines, the hunter's arrow, or even the bullet from a small caliber rifle.

During the next two days, Chelydra, the baby turtle, passed up many food items that she would later recognize as possible meals. Several schools of small rosyface shiners swam past, but the minnows were much too large and too fast for such a small turtle. By the fifth day after emerging from the sandy soil, Chelydra had metabolized all of the reserves from the yolk sac.

Early the next day, after the morning sun had climbed above the treetops, the turtle's attention was drawn to something crawling in the shallow water. Chelydra instinctively swam closer, and without thinking, without knowing what she was doing, without even realizing she was hungry, she suddenly extended her neck and opened her mouth and clamped her jaws shut. Chelydra had captured her first meal, with no direct help from anyone. Instinct and the knowledge inherited from many generations of ancestral turtles enabled her to pass this crucial test.

The baby turtle was holding a small worm in jaws superbly equipped for grabbing and holding squirming prey. Grasping the worm tightly, the turtle used her front feet and claws to tear at the worm, severing the worm into two pieces. Instinct again directed the little turtle, and she swallowed her first bite. The satisfying flavor of the worm further excited her and she turned her attention to the end of the worm that was wriggling on the sandy river bottom. Another sudden thrust of her head and clamping of her jaws and Chelydra completed her first meal. The torn worm had released its odors and activated the turtle's sense of smell. Turtles in the Blackwater River lived most of their lives in darkly stained water where most meals were detected by smell rather than by sight. Thus, the olfactory sense was more important to adult snapping turtles than was the sense of sight or touch or hearing.

Worms were an ideal food not just for baby turtles, but for baby snakes, baby lizards, and baby alligators. Upon hatching, these reptiles must independently learn to find, capture, and eat their food. Even the smallest turtle is capable of capturing worms, which provide the protein so essential for growth. Baby turtles could survive by eating only worms, but as adults they require bigger prey to satisfy their nutritional needs. Chelydra would eventually learn that there were many other foods available in the river where she lived.

From frogs and salamanders to lizards and turtles, immature animals that survive without parental guidance, must follow two basic rules of life: stay curious of all moving things smaller than they are and stay suspicious of all moving things larger than they are. Curiosity enables them to discover new foods through tasting small organisms. Suspicion enables them to avoid being killed and eaten through treating large organisms as potential predators.

During the next few weeks Chelydra tried unsuccessfully to capture many of the small animals along that stretch of riverbank. Small minnows were the most tempting target, but they were too quick for the baby turtle and she never managed to grasp one in her jaws. Crayfish were common on the river bottom and on the many rocks and roots that were such an integral part of the world of the baby turtle. Most crayfish were so large that Chelydra was more frightened than attracted to them. But small crayfish were also present and these were much more attractive to the hungry turtle. One day Chelydra spotted a tiny crayfish and instantly snapped her jaws shut around its tail. The crayfish reacted instinctively and its claws pinched the leg of the baby turtle. Hardly feeling this slight pinch, the turtle tightened her jaws. Using her front feet and claws, Chelydra quickly tore the small crayfish into pieces and thus learned about a second type of food. Although more difficult to capture than worms, crayfish were larger and more flavorful. Crayfish became her favorite target, and although she received many painful pinches none actually caused any serious damage to the little turtle.

Chelydra's home range was quite small, extending only sixty feet along the riverbank at the water's edge. She regularly moved back and forth along this stretch, expanding her world slowly. A small cove was located within this section of the river and was one of her favorite sites. The shallow water in the cove was slow moving and supported a dense stand of spikerush. Here Chelydra found both food and protection.

In late April, American toads migrated in mass to the river where they bred and later deposited thousands of eggs. Some of these toads shared the cove with Chelydra. By May, most breeding had been completed, and the baby turtle encountered many long, gelatinous strings of toad eggs incubating in the warm water. The toad eggs did not have an attractive odor and because they did not move they were not identified as potential food. During early May the eggs metamorphosed into embryonic tadpoles, and slight movements occurred within the gelatinous string that provided nourishment and protection to the toad embryos. By the middle of May the tadpoles were developed enough to free themselves from the gelatin that had been their home for three weeks, and the cove was soon alive with dense masses of thousands of wriggling toad tadpoles. These fed on algae, but remained motionless for long periods of time in the sixty-five degree water.

The movements of the feeding tadpoles attracted Chelydra and instinctively she snapped at one of the small black targets. The bulbous body, which was primarily stomach and tail at that stage, was a welcome new food. During the rest of May and into early June, Chelydra consumed dozens each day. The tadpoles gradually grew hind legs, and a few days later front legs appeared as the tail began to disappear. By late June, the toadlets had left the water and would not return until the following April when they, as adults, would instinctively move back into the Blackwater River for breeding.

Chelydra continued to feed on worms, crayfish, and tadpoles, but then experienced another valuable lesson. She was resting beside a large rock that was partially submerged along the river's edge when she spotted several small brown objects crawling almost imperceptibly along the surface of the rock. Some were almost as large as the head of the baby turtle, but a few were considerably smaller. She watched intently as they moved over the rock and then curiosity caused her to swim closer. The same instinct that enabled her to capture her first worm now caused her to snap at one of the small brown objects. She experienced her fourth food, a pond snail. The jaws of the young turtle had hardened somewhat since she emerged from the egg, and they easily crushed the snail shell.

One sunny July afternoon when Chelydra was nearly three months old she was resting under the roots of her favorite rhododendron, watching a small school of minnows cruising along in search of small invertebrates. Rhododendrons were in full bloom, with their pinkish-white flowers showcased by the background of waxy green leaves. Suddenly a bluish-black bird plunged into the water. The minnows darted wildly in all directions but one was injured and struggled awkwardly as blood seeped from a wound on its back. The minnow had been attacked by the belted kingfisher who frequented that stretch of the river in search of its daily meal of minnows. Chelydra had witnessed many similar dives and had been frightened each time the bird plunged into the river, even though the kingfisher had never actually attacked the baby turtle. After missing its target, the kingfisher flew up from the river and returned to its favorite branch on a yellow-barked river birch. From that perch it intently surveyed the river below for any careless minnow that ventured too close to the surface.

While watching the struggling minnow, Chelydra became aware of a fascinating pungent odor. Instinct caused the young female to associate the attractive odor with food, and she moved in its direction. That route took her directly toward the blood that was seeping from the fish. Within reach of the struggling minnow, the turtle immediately clamped her jaws around its tail. Utilizing the same successful technique of holding with her jaws and tearing with her front feet, she easily pulled loose a piece of fish. This food would become the staple of her diet throughout adult life.

Life was good for the young turtle during her first summer, as the waters of the Blackwater River warmed to comfortable temperatures near sixty-five degrees. The rhododendrons were almost done blooming and cones were forming on the hemlocks. An abundant diet of crayfish, worms, snails, and tadpoles contributed to the turtle's growth, but she still weighed less than one ounce. Chelydra became almost totally nocturnal, spending most of the daylight hours hidden along the shoreline of the river. She encountered many other residents of the river while searching for food, and learned to remain stationary when potential predators, such as mink and raccoon, approached. She also learned that many of the inhabitants were not predators, and she had little to fear from them. Muskrats swam lazily along the river's edge searching for succulent cutgrass, while green frogs sat motionless at the water's edge, vocalizing with their typical twanged rubber band calls. Female wood ducks led their broods cruising the fertile shoreline in search of invertebrates.

Several times Chelydra unsuccessfully attempted to capture minnows, but they were always too large and too quick for the inexperienced baby turtle. One day in late July Chelydra detected the same strong scent of minnow flesh and minnow blood that led to an unforgettable meal two months earlier. After quickly swimming eighteen feet upstream toward the scent, she found a minnow struggling in the water, another kingfisher victim. The scent of minnow and minnow blood meant the same thing to many animals that inhabited the Blackwater River—food. On that day the blood was detected by the only reptile, other than snapping turtles, that permanently inhabited the Blackwater River—a northern water snake. Nearly three feet long and six inches in circumference, the five-year old male snake regularly preyed on minnows, frogs, crayfish, and even small turtles. Only two months earlier the snake had captured and eaten a baby snapping turtle, one of Chelydra's sisters.

Six days earlier the snake had captured a small green frog, but that had been quickly digested and the snake was hungry again. The dark scaly reptile glided slowly and imperceptibly through the water. Upon reaching the minnow, the snake found the young turtle already eating. Water snakes were uncommon in the Blackwater River and Chelydra, never having encountered a large snake, was not experienced with this predator. She continued to tear off bites of minnow as the snake approached. Hesitant to give up the attractive food, the turtle did not have a chance to escape the sudden strike. The jaws of the snake were not as powerful as those of an adult snapping turtle, but they were armed with over forty sharp teeth adapted for grasping prey. The shell of the young turtle had hardened slightly and the short teeth of the snake did not penetrate, but they did hold firmly. Chelydra struggled violently but she could not pull loose. The snake moved its jaw to maneuver the small turtle so that it could be swallowed, but in so doing the sharp claws of the turtle scratched the eye of the snake. The reptile loosened its grasp just enough for Chelydra to escape and she quickly swam behind a rock and out of sight. Normally the snake would have pursued the small turtle and succeeded in making a meal of it, but the snake's attention was drawn to the minnow that drifted nearby in the water. Minnows were preferred over turtles and the snake's jaws soon encircled the minnow and maneuvered it head first into his throat. Chelydra would avoid these larger challengers, at least until she was old enough to defend herself from such a dangerous predator.

While moving along the river bank one evening, Chelydra was suddenly aware of another small turtle. This other turtle was actually one of her sisters from the same clutch of eggs that had hatched nearly four months earlier. Neither turtle recognized the other as a sibling. They did not fear one another, but were quite curious. They touched noses and then quietly swam around each other, smelling and touching as they moved.

Had they been young mammals such as squirrels, foxes, or deer, they probably would have played. Chases and mock fights would have taken place until they were too tired to continue. But most young reptiles never engage in play; such behavior typically does not occur in offspring not raised by their mother. Being cold-blooded, with their body temperature close to that of the surroundings, turtles are typically too sluggish to engage in play. They often remain immobile for hours (or even days) due to their extremely slow metabolism. Their small brains trigger action only when faced with challenges of eating or avoiding being eaten.

After a few minutes of close examination, the turtles separated and the second sister moved downstream. They would never see one another again. Two weeks later Chelydra's sister was eaten by a great blue heron that frequently waded through the shallow waters of the Blackwater River. Although the majestic six-foot tall heron typically preyed on minnows, frogs, and crayfish, occasionally it caught and consumed small rodents, small snakes, and small turtles.

Chelydra occasionally spotted an adult turtle moving slowly along the river's edge, but she remained motionless to avoid detection. She felt no urge to associate with another member of her species—even if the other turtle happened to be her mother. Instinct told her to avoid all large creatures. If she were to survive, any animal that was too large for her to eat must be viewed as a potential predator. Although Chelydra met a few other snapping turtles that summer, she met no other kind of turtles. Snapping turtles were the only resident species of aquatic turtle in the Blackwater River or in any of the streams, lakes, or beaver ponds throughout Canaan Valley. The box turtle, a terrestrial species, was the only other turtle that lived in the Valley, but it was quite rare.

This great Valley named Canaan, where the baby snapping turtle started her life was a wilderness unlike any other in the eastern United States. Situated in the Appalachian Mountains of West Virginia, this Valley was so inhospitable to humans that it contained no farms or settlements in 1886. One or two brave souls had attempted to settle in the Valley, but conditions were so harsh and intolerable that they were unable to establish permanent farms.

Though unwelcoming to humans, Canaan was one of the last sites in the east to support timber wolves and mountain lions plus elk and bison. The relatively flat Valley floor was located three thousand feet above sea level, while the mountains that surrounded the Valley were one thousand feet higher. The Canaan Valley watershed was four miles wide and nearly fourteen miles long. Over fifty miles of rivers and streams drained the thirty-six-thousand-acre Valley. The Blackwater River flowed north through the Valley then turned west and cut between Brown Mountain and Canaan Mountain before dropping through Blackwater Canyon.

Few reptiles of any type lived in Canaan Valley. Lizards were rare and only a few species of snakes were able to survive the severe climate of this unique valley. The smooth green snake, redbelly snake, ringneck snake, garter snake, and northern water snake were present, although relatively scarce. Along the eastern border of Canaan Valley, an occasional timber rattlesnake wandered from Dolly Sods onto the rocky ridges of Cabin Mountain. Rattlesnakes, however, never ventured down onto the Valley floor.

August brought low water levels to the Blackwater River that year, as the monthly rainfall dropped to slightly less than two inches. Chelydra was forced to leave the small cove where she had spent much of the summer. Oxygen levels dropped and the baby turtle crawled deep under the rhododendron roots. Her appetite declined and eating almost stopped. By the end of August she had entered a state of torpor, and remained inactive through September.

Chelydra had passed the two biggest tests that young turtles face during their first year; she had learned to obtain food and had learned to avoid becoming food herself. Now she faced another situation that could bring her short life to an early end.

Snow flurries fell during September and the bracken ferns that covered the natural openings along the riverbank were killed by the first frost. Water temperature dropped and instinctively Chelydra responded. She did not know that temperatures would drop below zero during the next few months or that thick ice would cover the Blackwater River. She could not follow her mother into a warm den as did the black bear cubs that frequented Canaan Valley. Her actions occurred without reason, guided only by instincts passed down through thousands of years of experience gained by her ancestors.

One day during the first week of October Chelydra entered a small stream flowing into the river from an adjacent bog. The water in the stream was reddish-black due to the tannic acid and iron from the bog. This stream and hundreds of others flowing from bogs throughout Canaan Valley were responsible for the color of the Blackwater River. Water from the bog was much cooler and more oxygenated than that of the river and carried with it many interesting odors. Chelydra reached a small thicket of speckled alder and explored the many openings and depressions through which water flowed. She spent the next few days in the flooded alder thicket. During the fourth night she burrowed into a depression beneath the roots of large alder. Satisfied with the stream of richly-oxygenated water flowing past her and the shelter of the roots overhead, Chelydra partially settled into the mud to commence the first of many long hibernations that would guarantee her survival through the winters that characterized Canaan Valley.

From the original thirty-two eggs, only two snapping turtle hatchlings had survived the first year of life. Luck and inherited survival skills had enabled these two to survive the period of greatest vulnerability. They would face many threats before they reached adulthood, but no other year would pose as many dangers as did the first year of their lives.

CHAPTER THREE

1887:
LOGGING

Chelydra's first true winter of hibernation passed with no life-threatening events. Her instincts had directed her to an excellent site with all the prerequisites for hibernation. The roots of the alder provided protection against predators and the moving water remained just above freezing. Because her metabolism came nearly to a stop she needed only small amounts of oxygen, and the moving water provided that.

Chelydra was never more dependent on her instincts than during hibernation. She had enjoyed numerous opportunities to learn what foods to eat, but only one brief opportunity to select an adequate hibernaculum. Fortunately, she had inherited the knowledge that dictated when and where to hibernate.

Chelydra remained under the alder roots through the long winter months while ice covered the river and snow accumulated throughout the forest. She did not eat during the six months of inactivity. What little nourishment she needed was absorbed from the fat reserves accumulated the previous summer. By late March water temperatures increased slightly, but snow and ice were still present on the surrounding mountains. The stream where she hibernated originated on Canaan Mountain, flowed into a bog, and then left the bog to become a stream once again.

Although spring had officially arrived during March, several late season snowfalls and temperatures near zero in early April created the appearance of winter. But warm rains during the second week of April melted most of the snow and ice, and the water flowing over and around Chelydra warmed to nearly forty degrees. Although still in a state of torpor she sensed the change, and over a period of five days she began to move. She changed position under the roots and extended her neck so that her nostrils were above the water. The warm rains continued and by the third week of April Chelydra abandoned the alder roots and moved to the Blackwater River.

Chelydra's metabolism increased as water temperature increased. Her first and most important urge was to find food. Although she had successfully obtained food during her first summer, her diet had been rather restricted. The actions and movements of organisms such as worms and crayfish and minnows immediately identified them as potential prey to Chelydra. Other foods were not so easily identified; this was especially true of plant materials. Chelydra was primarily a carnivore but would ultimately become an omnivore, eating both plant and animal foods. She learned of the edibility of plant matter in several ways. During her first year of life, she had accidentally torn off and swallowed pieces of vegetation while catching small crayfish that were clinging to the stems of pondweeds. After a few such incidents she intentionally began to bite off the ends of succulent young leaves and thus these became a regular part of her diet.

During late June of the second year of life she noticed several small, round, purplish objects rolling slowly along the river bottom. Curiosity led her to snap at one and in so doing she experienced her first taste of fruit. Although not so enjoyable as minnow flesh, the berries were certainly much easier to catch and Chelydra ate two of them. These were serviceberries, also known as June berries and shadberries, depending on the region of the country where they were growing. Serviceberry trees, being intolerant of shade, grew in openings where they received full sunlight during most of the daylight hours. Branches overhanging the Blackwater River released overripe berries into the shallow water along the riverbank. Being the first fruit to mature each year, before blackberries or blueberries or black cherries or viburnum fruits, they were prized by many birds and mammals. Cedar waxwings and robins, ruffed grouse and wild turkey, deer mice and red squirrels, raccoons and black bear, all relished the sweet, juicy fruits.

Canaan Valley, and especially its wetlands, pulsed with animal activities during April and May as amphibians and birds produced a constant chorus of breeding calls. In contrast, the reptiles and mammals were relatively quiet, except for the snort of a deer or the tail slap of a beaver. Whereas reptiles were rare in and around the Blackwater River, mammals were much more abundant than their calls and sounds indicated. Beaver, muskrats, mink, raccoons, and river otter were important members of Chelydra's river ecosystem. All of these mid-sized mammals left some type of sign along the riverbank. Their presence was not reflected by their calls, but their sign was an excellent indicator of their abundance. Tracks of each could be easily identified by size or shape or tail drag. Both beavers and muskrats dug bank dens; beaver dens were twice the size of muskrat dens. They were located at water's edge so that the aquatic rodents could swim directly into the den. Beaver and river otter advertised their territories by making scent stations along the bank; both rodents could thus be easily detected and identified by all resident mammals. Unlike the nauseating scent of the Valley's striped skunks, the sweet odor produced by the scent glands of beaver was so powerful and permeating that even the weak olfactory senses of humans could detect it from several feet away.

River otters left other sign to confirm their presence. The most playful of all mammals in the Valley, they spent many idle hours sliding down the riverbank into the water. Each beaver and muskrat had its favorite feeding station, and they would sit along the water's edge and eat their favorite foods—succulent, herbaceous plants for the muskrat and the tender bark of woody stems for the beaver. Raccoons often left their middens, piles of clamshells, where they had enjoyed an evening meal "on the half-shell".

Other mammals left no obvious sign, and their presence often went unnoticed, even by ever-alert young snapping turtles. One small mouse-like mammal was present in the small side streams, but seldom ventured out into the Blackwater River. It was the water shrew, an excellent swimmer that spends its entire life in or at the edge of the water.

Although several species of shrews frequented the coniferous forests of Canaan, and ventured close to the water shrew's territory this was the only aquatic form. Short-tailed shrews were the largest and most abundant of all shrews present in inhabited forests, fields, and wetlands. The masked shrew was the most abundant shrew of the wetland forests, while smoky and pygmy shrews preferred the mosses and litter of the forest floor. All the shrews were carnivorous, daily consuming small animals equal to their own body-weight. Worms, beetles, snails, caterpillars, salamanders, and baby mice were included in their diets. Quick, aggressive, and ever hungry, shrews were very efficient hunters.

Chelydra had nothing to fear from any of these shrews. Even the water shrew, which was somewhat longer than Chelydra, weighed less than one ounce. Although water shrews were not predators of small turtles, they were competitors for many of the same animal foods targeted by the young turtle—crayfish, minnows, snails, and worms. Water shrews were much more adept at pursuing and capturing minnows and swimming insects than were turtles. Chelydra could not chase down and catch minnows, but instead had to lie in wait until an unsuspecting small fish swam by.

The young turtle regularly observed several nocturnal mammals, although she never had direct contact with them. As dusk settled over the river, Chelydra observed bats, the only true flying mammals, as they emerged from their daytime retreats and began their nighttime foraging. Like shrews bats possess an extremely high metabolism, consuming large numbers of insects. Over Chelydra's stretch of the Blackwater River, swarms of insects attracted colorful species such as red bats and hoary bats. Feeding over water, they raised their young under tree bark or in hollow trees.

Chelydra occasionally watched another flying mammal, although flying in name only. The northern flying squirrel, a nocturnal rodent, spent its days in tree dens or leaf nests high in the towering red spruce so common along the river bottom. Although their activity periods were similar to bats, their feeding behavior was quite different. The northern flying squirrel was primarily a vegetarian, consuming underground fungi, lichens, tree buds, and fruits. Occasionally they added insects, snails, and bird eggs to their diet. Although the flying squirrel could not actually fly, a wide web of skin between the front legs and hind legs enabled it to glide more than one hundred feet. Climbing to the top of a large spruce it would launch itself away from the tree and sail gracefully through the forest to another tree. Although Chelydra showed little interest in these nighttime gliders, they did regularly cross the Blackwater River.

The northern flying squirrel was a relict species of the Ice Age, that geological period when northern boreal forests covered much of West Virginia. At that time, conifers such as red spruce and balsam fir were the dominant forest cover type over much of the central Appalachians. Although the great glaciers advanced no further south than central Pennsylvania, they dictated the climate of West Virginia and Canaan Valley. During that time, the northern flying squirrel was common throughout West Virginia. As the glaciers receded and the Ice Age came to an end, the climate of the central Appalachians moderated. Red spruce and balsam firs were not able to survive the warmer climates and were replaced by oak, maple, basswood, and yellow poplar. Only at the higher elevations did red spruce and balsam fir survive. And likewise only at the higher elevations did the northern flying squirrel survive. By 1880, this relict of the Ice Age remained in only six mountainous counties in West Virginia. Canaan Valley, with its huge expanse of northern coniferous forests, offered excellent habitat for this small mammal.

During the breeding season, the assortment of vocalizations that filled the air was an excellent measure of wildlife abundance and diversity. Each frog and toad and each songbird had a unique call or song to identify that particular species. Chelydra did not hear many of the bird songs that filled the forest during May mornings; the sounds did not penetrate the waters of the Blackwater River. However, after darkness had settled over the Valley and Chelydra began her nightly food searches, the night sounds surrounded her. She was familiar with the calls of spring peepers, American toads, and green frogs that shared the river along with the saw-whet and barred owls that nested in nearby trees. Those calls were a normal part of her environment and she neither enjoyed nor feared them. She had no way to know which animal produced the calls, just as she was unable to identify the mixture of other sounds occurring at night.

Sounds produced by animals in the Blackwater River were of great interest, however, as her survival depended on identifying the animal that produced each sound. She acquired acute awareness of changes in water pressure and wave patterns as animals swam or waded in the Blackwater River. Because she could not distinguish between a harmless beaver and a life-threatening raccoon or between a white sucker and a water snake, she avoided them all.

By August a deceptive quietness had settled over the Valley. The total wildlife population had swelled many times greater than that of the previous April, as the yearly production of offspring was nearly completed. But the youngsters and their parents were quiet, having no reason to announce their presence. There were a few calls from green frogs and an occasional call from juvenile barred owls, but nothing compared to the constant chorus during May and June.

The summer serenity was broken one day in early August by several loud crashes that originated some distance down river. Although Chelydra did not actually hear the crashes she felt the vibrations that moved through the forest floor and into the waters of the Blackwater River. Because they were some distance away, the sounds were of no concern to her. But as the days passed the unusual crashes came closer, causing Chelydra and most other Blackwater wildlife to react fearfully as the shock waves passed through the bed of the river.

By the end of August, the crashes were so close to Chelydra's home that some of the other wildlife had moved upstream. First to go was the great blue heron, followed a few days later by the barred owls and ravens and goshawks that had nested along the river. The white-tailed deer, black bears, and bobcats could not tolerate the disturbance and they too moved upstream toward Sand Run and the North Branch of the Blackwater. The larger animals that depended on the coniferous forest for food and shelter were forced to leave, but the habitats of those living in the Blackwater were not directly affected. Thus, Chelydra and the beaver, muskrat, mink, and other aquatic species continued life as usual.

Giant trees crashing to the forest floor caused the disturbing sounds. Teams of loggers with crosscut saws over six feet in length were systematically cutting all red spruce and hemlocks in a narrow band along the Blackwater River. The logging operations had begun several years earlier and slowly worked their way up the Blackwater from Davis. By the end of 1887 they reached the junction where Sand Run joined the Blackwater River.

By the third week of September Chelydra once again felt a familiar urge to migrate up the small stream that entered the Blackwater River. As if drawn by a magnet, she moved to the same alder where she had hibernated the previous year, and promptly began to dig deep under its roots. She had survived another year, entering the relatively safe state of hibernation with little to fear. Her world was changing, however, and it would never again resemble that of her mother or the other snapping turtles of the Canaan Valley ecosystem.

CHAPTER FOUR

1888: LOG FLOATS

Most young snapping turtles entered hibernation at the same time as Chelydra. A few weeks later the older, larger turtles began to leave the river and search for their favorite hibernacula up the nearby tributaries. Not all turtles in Canaan Valley selected the type of hibernaculum used by Chelydra. While most turtles chose protected pockets under the roots of an alder growing along the bank of a small stream, a few turtles chose sites located within the dam of a beaver pond, a location that provided the two key features necessary for survival—moving water and predator protection.

At the end of the 1800s, beaver were rare throughout Canaan Valley because of the scarcity of aspen, their preferred food. Mature forests of spruce, hemlock, and fir did not provide the sustenance needed by beaver, which can reach weights of sixty pounds and need several pounds of bark each day. Despite the food limitation, a few beaver families had established residence in the Valley. One site where they had settled was near the mouth of Sand Run, just upstream from the Blackwater River. This family of parents with their single offspring constructed a dam across Sand Run and dug a den deep into the steep bank. Beaver build three types of dens: free-standing lodges, bank dens, and bank lodges built over the opening of a bank den. Because of the steep banks along the lower reaches of Sand Run, this family constructed a bank den, then for extra protection built a bank lodge over its entrance. Although aspen trees were few and scattered along Sand Run, the hemlock, black cherry, and alder provided just enough bark to support this one small family.

If an abundant supply of aspen had been available, this family unit would have consisted of six members: a set of parents, two yearlings from the previous summer, and two youngsters from the current summer. Lacking adequate food to nourish the entire family through the extended winter months, the female had produced only one young the previous year and none in 1888.

The engineering skills of these large rodents were crucial not only for building the den that protected them from severe weather and predators, but also for constructing the dam and food cache. The few beaver to establish residence along the deeper pools of the Blackwater River did not construct dams—there was no need. The primary purpose of a dam is to create a deep pond of water that will not freeze solid in winter. Beaver do not hibernate, but instead feed throughout the winter months on the food cache they store for just that purpose. Sand Run was less than twenty feet wide near its mouth and the beaver selected a site where the high banks enabled them to build a dam with a minimum of effort. As water levels rose and reached the top of the dam, the beaver added more logs and mud until the final dam was nearly forty feet wide and over six feet high. The resulting pond covered nearly an acre, an area large enough to ensure the survival of the beaver through the hazards of winter.

Beginning in October, the beaver family worked harder and longer than at any other time of the year. They constantly repaired the dam so that it could withstand the heavy rainfall and snowmelt that could threaten the safety of their pond during the winter months. The adults had acquired many of their skills through instinct and experience, but lessons from their parents were the most valuable. These rodents were social animals and had endless opportunities to observe their elders.

Just as important to the beaver family as the dam was their food cache, the food reserves that were stored in the pond. Tree cutting reached a peak during October and November when they needed logs for their dam, branches for their bank lodge, and food for their food cache. Small trees and the limbs from larger trees were hauled to the deepest part of the beaver pond where they were stored in a large pile. This pile extended from the bottom of the pond to the water surface and was nearly twenty-five feet wide. The pond froze over in November, and deep snow soon covered the hillsides above Sand Run. Winter had arrived and the beaver would not remember the warm, sunny days of autumn as they faced the challenge of ice, snow, darkness, and cold. Survival depended on the strength of the dam and on the huge pile of branches that formed the food cache. The winter days were spent sleeping and eating, and occasionally repairing a leak in the dam. Several times each day the beaver would swim out of their den to the food cache, cut off a small section of tree branch, haul it back into the den, and then leisurely chew off the bark that provided the nutrition essential to their survival.

One of the adult turtles who typically hibernated in a beaver dam was Chelydra's mother. One night in early October she left that stretch of the Blackwater River where she had spent the summer and moved about four hundred yards up Sand Run until she came to a beaver dam. Under cover of darkness, she easily moved around the end of the dam and swam out into the quiet pond that had formed behind the wall of mud, sticks, and small logs. Swimming slowly underwater, she moved deliberately back and forth along the upstream side of the dam. Finally she stopped and began digging purposefully into the dam. She had located her destination, a site where water slowly leaked through from the pond behind the dam.

Beaver are excellent engineers, but their dams are not constructed to be totally leak-proof. Beaver plug all large leaks, but the small ones are ignored; perhaps they realize that small leaks assist in relieving pressure on the dam when heavy rainfall causes the water level to rise.

With considerable effort, the large female turtle pulled her twenty-nine pounds between the logs and limbs used by the beaver family to construct their dam. About halfway into the dam she stopped and turned so that her head was facing upstream toward the pond and after a few minor adjustments she settled into the position where she would remain throughout winter. The water flowing slowly over and around her body would not freeze and would provide all the oxygen needed during the six months that she would remain in hibernation. She was quite safe from predators, possibly more than those turtles that hibernated under the roots of alders along the tributaries of the Blackwater River.

Hibernation in beaver dams was not without risk. Heavy rains, combined with rapid snowmelt, often created flood waters that washed out dams in the larger streams. But such flood events, which typically occurred during March, rarely caused deaths. Any turtles washed downstream simply dug into the bank under the roots of a streamside tree and spent the last month of their hibernation in the emergency hibernaculum. Occasionally an unusually large flood washed a turtle far downstream, but the turtle would return to its normal stretch of stream within a few months after leaving hibernation.

Unbeknownst to the beaver family, theirs was not the only dam on Sand Run. In August, when water levels were low, loggers had moved into the Sand Run watershed; their goal was to build dams. By the end of October they had built four splash dams along the upper half of Sand Run and three holding ponds along the lower half. The splash dams were designed to create a pool of water that would be released later to aid in floating logs downstream. The holding ponds were designed to temporarily store logs, with shorelines for stacking tall piles of logs that would be tumbled into the flood waters that moved past.

Chelydra's mother was unaware of the activities occurring along Sand Run while she was safely encased within the beaver dam. The logging industry had discovered the enormous timber resources of Canaan Valley in 1885 and during the winter months of 1887, while Chelydra's mother peacefully avoided the cold and wind and snow and ice, loggers worked continuously felling the valuable timber trees along that stretch of Sand Run. The main logging crew had moved into Sand Run during September. Four crews, six men each, began cutting the dense stands of hemlock and red spruce along Sand Run, while three more crews were cutting the tall straight black cherry on the sandy ridges above Sand Run.

Sounds of axes and crosscut saws filled the watershed from daylight till dark. Trees near the stream were felled first, then those uphill from Sand Run. Although the cold temperatures created hardships for the loggers, this was the season when logs could best be moved. The ice and snow and frozen ground made it possible for logs to be hauled from the surrounding hillsides to the banks of Sand Run. The huge logs were skidded by teams of sturdy draft horses and by even more powerful teams of huge oxen.

The banks of Sand Run upstream from the beaver dam were lined with the massive trunks of trees, many of which extended into the water. These were not entire trees, but only the straight, limbless lower sections. The tops and branches had been removed and only the logs remained. The fall rains partially filled the splash dams and holding dams and many logs were rolled into the ponds. When they would hold no more, logs were carefully stacked along the water's edge.

The West Virginia Central Railroad had reached the town of Davis in 1884, a result of the efforts of Henry Gassaway Davis. An engine house, a depot, and a hotel were constructed in 1885, and in 1886 a sawmill was erected along the banks of the Blackwater River.

New England, along with many cities and towns of the Atlantic coast, was growing rapidly and such growth required lumber for houses and businesses. Canaan Valley and the hillsides of the Blackwater watershed supported one of the greatest remaining concentrations of timber east of the Mississippi River. The black cherry, balsam fir, red spruce, and eastern hemlock were so abundant and so valuable that sawmills, pulp mills, and tanneries at Davis ran nearly continuously from 1886 till 1924. Over 50,000 carloads of lumber were hauled over the mountain by railroad to Cumberland, Maryland during that period. The boomtown of Davis exploded in size to 3,200 inhabitants, as schools, churches, hotels, restaurants, saloons, and stores were quickly built to support the workers who were so essential to the lumber industry.

Timber near Davis and the sawmills was cut first. After the forests immediately surrounding Davis had been cleared, the loggers slowly expanded their operations up the Blackwater River, cutting trees in a narrow swath on each side. By 1887 most trees along the Blackwater River from Davis to Sand Run and beyond to the North Branch had been logged and floated to the mills.

By February 1888, over four thousand logs, many three feet in diameter, lined the banks of Sand Run. Many were in the water and some had been rolled or skidded onto the ice. The logs themselves created dams that, along with the splash dams and holding dams and one beaver dam, created a series of pools extending more than one mile up Sand Run from the mouth of the Blackwater River. Water from each dam backed up to the base of the next upstream dam, resulting in a nearly continuous body of water from the mouth of the Blackwater.

The water behind the dams had frozen in late December and was several feet thick by the end of February. But March brought unusually warm weather and heavy rainfall. The snow, which was over seven feet deep in many places, began to melt and added to the heavy runoff that was quickly raising water levels in the Blackwater River and its many tributaries throughout Canaan Valley. As these waters entered Sand Run they began melting the ice that had formed behind the numerous dams. Although floods were seldom desirable, they were exactly what the loggers needed. Floodwaters would float the thousands of logs that lined the banks of Sand Run down to the mills at Davis.

Two loggers were brought from Maine where log floats had been used for many years to move logs from woods to mills. The men were experienced in building the crucial splash dams, but were also experienced in setting the dynamite charges at the bases of these same dams that would initiate the carefully orchestrated and essential flood. With the dams overflowing and ice melting, the first charge of dynamite was exploded during the last week of March. The first splash dam quickly gave way and the mass of ice and water and logs began inching its way down Sand Run. Dozens of loggers watched as it pushed downstream. At almost the exact same time this wall reached the second splash dam, a second charge of dynamite was exploded. The size of the floodwaters immediately doubled and increased in speed as they rumbled toward the third splash dam. Again, a carefully timed explosion weakened the log dam enough so that it gave way to the tremendous power that was surging into its ponded waters.

The floodwaters, hindered by the ice and logs, actually moved somewhat slowly, but move they did. Most of the stacked logs were swept from the banks as the waters pushed downstream. Any logs that failed to move were rolled into the floodwaters by the nearly fifty men who were stationed along the banks of Sand Run. The men were equipped with log peaveys, cant hooks, and pike poles to assure that the majority of the logs would be swept from Sand Run into the Blackwater River. A log peavey is a heavy pole nearly six feet in length, with a pointed metal end and a steel hook for rolling logs. A cant hook is similar, but shorter and lighter, with a steel lip rather than a spike at its end. Pike poles are twelve to twenty feet in length, with a spike on the end, used to maneuver logs as they float downstream.

The rain continued and water levels increased until the entire force of the log mass approached the last dam before reaching the Blackwater River. All other dams had been obliterated and this one small beaver dam had no chance of remaining intact.

The first sign of danger reached the beaver family through the vibrations caused by the dynamite exploding at the base of the splash dam located more than one mile upstream. After nearly two hours they felt the ground shake as dynamite destroyed the second dam, and several hours later they felt the explosion at the third splash dam. Then all was quiet. Although somewhat disturbed, the beaver did not feel any urge to leave the safety of their den.

Typically, beaver had little to fear from rising waters. They could easily swim out of their den and move to higher ground when floods occurred. After waters receded they would return to their pond, rebuild the dam, and continue life as normal. This time was different, quite different. The beaver den consisted of a long tunnel that began at water level, continued seven feet into the bank then curved upward for three feet before ending in the five-foot wide cavern that was the actual home shared by the entire family.

Nearly eight hours after feeling the first dynamite explosion, the ice of the frozen beaver pond began to creak and groan as pressure of the rising waters reached the frozen pond. The beaver family in their bank den immediately detected these alarming changes. The adult male swam out to investigate, but the adult female and the lone yearling remained in the warm, dark, security of their den. The two adults had mated earlier in the year and the fifty-five pound female was carrying two young. Gestation period was 128 days and the birth of the two kits, as young beaver are called, would occur in May.

The floodwaters that swept into the beaver dam raised so rapidly that the adult male could not swim back into the den; huge blocks of ice forced him to leave the pond and try to escape. The den tunnel and then the cavern were quickly filled to the ceiling. The adult female swam to the den entrance but the mass of ice and logs that swept past were so threatening that she retreated back into the den and began frantically digging into the ceiling. Although a beaver can remain under water for nearly ten minutes that was not enough time for her to dig above the water level and reach the life-giving air. The den was constructed so that its thick walls and ceiling would provide insulation from the below zero temperatures that were so common throughout the long winter. This barrier to the cold, so essential for survival, was also escape-proof. Death came quickly, first the yearling with its smaller lung capacity, then the adult female with her two unborn young.

Chelydra's mother was unaware of the wall of floodwater that was bearing down on her. The small dam was constructed to withstand normal spring runoff, but this was not normal. The floodwaters never slowed as they smashed through the beaver dam. There was no warning and the dam suddenly disintegrated. The mud, branches, and logs that had been so carefully positioned by the beaver were swept downstream. And with them went Chelydra's mother. The mother turtle would have been able to survive a normal flood, but there was nothing normal about the wall of ice and logs and mud and water that destroyed the beaver dam. The turtle was caught in the melee and swept downstream before she had a chance to react. Few animals could survive such an onslaught and the aquatic life along the lower reaches of Sand Run would be greatly reduced by the man-made flood that was designed to move logs to the sawmills in Davis.

By design, the floodwaters moved rather slowly, with nearly forty-eight hours passing before the floodwaters started to recede. During that time the logging crews were working feverishly to roll logs into Sand Run before water levels dropped too low to float a log. Loggers with their long pike poles and corked boots kept the logs moving downriver until they were stopped by the booms of chains and logs stretched across the river at Davis. There the logs were held until they could be directed into the mill where the giant band saws would convert them into lumber.

CHAPTER FIVE

1889-1900: MORE LOGGING AND LOG FLOATS

The flood waters that imperiled the beaver family and Chelydra's mother did not impact Chelydra's hibernaculum because it was located in a small side tributary somewhat upstream of the mouth of Sand Run. During the weeks immediately following the flood, signs of spring gradually appeared throughout Canaan Valley. Temperatures slowly increased, as the spans of long nights and short days gradually became equal. Whereas the nights were nearly fourteen hours long during December, by March the hours of darkness had shortened to only twelve hours. In contrast, daylength was slowly increasing and the twelve hours of daylight were triggering the first obvious signs of spring in the waters and woods of Canaan Valley. While black bears and groundhogs and snapping turtles were still safely protected by their hibernacula, a few hibernating animals had begun to respond to the lengthening days and increasing temperatures.

Wood frogs were the first of the winter hibernators to advertise their emergence. A few warm days in March triggered the movements of wood frogs from their winter hibernacula under leaves and logs on the forest floor to the few isolated ponds and pools that had open water. The dark waters of these shallow pools had been warmed by the sun and became the temporary home to thousands of noisy wood frogs. Although their quacking calls resembled those of ducks more than frogs, the clamor served its purpose of attracting female wood frogs to the breeding ponds. A thin layer of ice skimmed over the top of the ponds during many nights of the March-April breeding season, but the frogs simply buried into the mud and muck of the pond bottom and emerged when sunlight again warmed the water.

To humans, wood frogs are one of the most attractive of all frogs inhabiting Canaan Valley. Their alluring pinkish-tan coloration enables them to blend in with the leaves of the forest floor, while the black mask, which extends from the shoulder through the eye and to the snout, serves to break up their outline, as do the facial masks of many other animals.

Breeding was completed by mid-April and the result was millions of eggs deposited in the many small ponds that dotted the floor of Canaan Valley. Each small temporary pool was visited by over three hundred female wood frogs and each produced an egg mass that contained up to three thousand eggs. The egg masses were all deposited at a communal site in the middle of the pond, resulting in a singular gelatinous body of nearly one million eggs. Those egg masses in the center remained ten degrees warmer than the actual water temperature and as a result the central masses had a greater chance of hatching than did the outer masses.

The adult frogs gradually left the pond, and three weeks after the primary egg mass was completed the first wriggling, squirming black tadpoles appeared. They emerged from the egg mass over a two-week period until the last had wriggled free of the communal incubator. Thousands did not hatch, primarily those on the outside of the mass, but by the first of May each pond was alive with hundreds of thousands of half-inch long tadpoles. They fed on algae during the next two months until hind legs appeared and the tail disappeared. By early July the small froglets crawled out of the black water and scattered throughout the forest where they and the other forest amphibians consumed huge numbers of nutritious snails, spiders, and insects that lived under the logs and leaf litter of the forest floor.

Unlike green frogs and pickerel frogs, which were permanent residents of Canaan Valley beaver ponds and streams, wood frogs were not truly aquatic species and spent only a few weeks of their adult life in water. Although most newly-developed wood froglets would not survive their first year, the following March would again manifest the first sign of spring as the ephemeral pools of Canaan Valley provided temporary, but essential, homes to thousands of calling wood frogs.

Chelydra knew nothing of calling wood frogs, or of their eggs or tadpoles. She knew nothing of the events of the log float down Sand Run and the Blackwater River. The mating calls of the wood frogs had ceased by the time she emerged from her hibernaculum and she never ventured into the ephemeral ponds that were so essential to the future of wood frogs. These woodland amphibians rarely entered the Blackwater River and those that did were present prior to the time Chelydra emerged from hibernation.

Although totally submerged under the roots of an alder shrub and covered by six inches of water Chelydra subconsciously detected the lengthening daylight hours. By early April, the increase in water temperatures and daylength prompted her to stir within her hibernaculum. She crawled upward through the alder roots until she could project her nostrils above the surface of the small stream of water that had protected her during the long winter months. Although the oxygen in the air was quite welcome, the temperatures were not high enough to entice her to leave the site and she retreated to the safety of her hibernaculum. Two days later she again felt the urge to move, and that time the air temperatures were warm enough to entice her to swim a short distance down the small stream. Another year thus began for Chelydra, but she was facing challenges that her immediate ancestors had never faced—challenges so threatening that her very survival was at stake. That year would be more traumatic than any Chelydra or any other inhabitant of the Blackwater River had ever faced.

When Chelydra finally reached the Blackwater River after

three days of slowly meandering down the small stream where her hibernaculum was located, she encountered a scene never witnessed by any snapping turtle in the Blackwater River. The riverbanks were barren. The hemlocks, red spruce, viburnums, rhododendrons, and alder that had been there when she entered hibernation were gone. Her favorite refugia under the roots of streamside trees had been totally destroyed and nothing familiar remained. A few giant logs in the river and along the bank were so lodged that neither the rushing waters nor the loggers with their pike poles and peaveys had been able to pry them loose. The logs that greeted Chelydra when she entered the Blackwater River were not a serious impediment to her movements, but they had certainly altered her environment. Snapping turtles do not eat during the first two or three weeks after leaving hibernation, but spend most of the daylight hours in shallow water where the spring sunshine slowly warms the water. Because turtles are cold-blooded, with body temperatures similar to that of the water in which they live, they remain relatively inactive until water temperatures exceed fifty degrees.

Chelydra moved slowly along the river's edge in search of shallow coves where the water would be warmer than that in the main channel of the river. At the mouth of one cove she was stopped by a large spruce log that was lodged in the exposed roots of a stream side birch. She had easily worked her way around the log and was entering the cove when her attention was drawn to several large black birds along the riverbank. They were even larger than the black ravens she had learned to avoid after she barely escaped the grasp of one while moving with her hatchling sisters from her birth nest to the river.

The birds were turkey vultures, scavengers referred to as buzzards by the local loggers. They were not the least bit interested in Chelydra or any other animal that swam past them that day. The flood of logs and ice and high water had provided the scavengers with numerous meals in the carcasses of animals that had been drowned or crushed, including a large beaver and a small deer. The vultures that Chelydra had spotted were feeding on the carcass of a large snapping turtle. They had first pecked out its eyeballs, then pulled out pieces of the intestines through the cracks in the shell caused by crushing logs. All that remained of the once-impressive relict of the dinosaur age were an eyeless skull, a crushed shell, and shrunken legs and tail. The curved beaks of the vultures, which were designed for removing meat from a carcass, had efficiently transferred the flesh of the dead snapping turtle into their own bodies; to be converted into turkey vulture flesh.

After the vultures had removed the last bits of muscle and tissue from inside the shell and had moved off in search of another flood-killed meal, Chelydra swam close to the remains. She recognized it as a snapping turtle, but had no way to know that the empty shell was the last vestige of the individual responsible for her very existence. She had never seen her mother, had never formed any attachment to her, and thus would have felt no loss had she known the remains were those of her mother.

Although the appearance of the Blackwater River had changed drastically, life resumed for the crayfish and water snakes, the kingfishers and great blue herons, and even the snapping turtles who called this section of Canaan Valley their home. The bed and banks of Sand Run and the Blackwater River slowly recovered, as seedlings of alder and viburnum, aspen and birch, and spruce and hemlock appeared. Although heavy rainstorms deposited silt in the streams, the overall water quality of Sand Run and the Blackwater River was suitable to support nearly as many crayfish and minnows and brook trout as had occurred prior to the log float.

Chelydra spent the next few summers in the Blackwater River, where the size of her home range increased along with her own body size. The spring floods of 1892, however, swept a few logs into that section of the Blackwater that Chelydra called home, and by summer logs were scattered throughout that section of the River. All logs that could be economically cut and skidded to Sand Run had been removed the previous year, and no further logging was conducted in the Sand Run watershed that year. However, there still remained several large tracts of virgin forests in the upper end of Canaan Valley, and the logging camps were moved to the Mill Run and Club Run area.

From 1892 to 1894, loggers continued to cut the conifers throughout that portion of Canaan Valley that seventy years later would become Canaan Valley State Park. By 1894 the Blackwater River was so full of logs that most aquatic animals had been forced to leave or had died. Hemlock and spruce logs began to pile up in the River from Club Run to Davis, a distance of nearly twenty-five miles.

Chelydra spent the winter of 1894-1895 in the same tributary where she had hibernated every winter of her life. Upon emerging from hibernation in April 1895, however, conditions were so inhospitable in the Blackwater River that she struggled to survive. The scarcity of food was quite serious, and on many days she could not find enough food to satisfy her hunger. Numbers of crayfish, minnows, and snails were greatly reduced due to the logging.

Chelydra's search for food brought her to the mouth of Sand Run, where she soon discovered that the supply of minnows, crayfish, and worms was notably better than that in the Blackwater River. Because logging had not been continued in the Sand Run watershed, the quality of water flowing out of Sand Run was much higher than that in the Blackwater River. The attractive odors of potential food flowing down Sand Run told her where the best living conditions occurred and by the end of summer she had abandoned the Blackwater River and established her new home in the lower reaches of Sand Run.

Logging continued in the southern end of Canaan Valley around the headwaters of the Blackwater River during the remainder of the 1890s. Over one hundred thousand logs were floated down the Blackwater to the mills in Davis during 1899 and 1900. The massive flow of logs down the River had no effect on Chelydra, but of those animals living in the area, only the turkey vultures benefited.

The log-floats that took place on the Blackwater River between 1885 and 1900 caused the deaths of several beaver, deer, muskrats, mink, river otter, and snapping turtles, plus even a few humans. Yet an occasional snapping turtle did somehow survive in each of the major waters of Canaan Valley; in the North Branch, the Little Blackwater, Yoakum Run, Mill Run, Freeland Run, Glade Run, and even in the Blackwater itself. Snapping turtles had historically endured conditions much more severe than those resulting from the calamitous logging in Canaan Valley, and would most likely face many more before their species disappeared from the planet Earth.

No new log floats would ever again take place on Sand Run. Nearly ninety years would pass before the timber growing along the banks would be large enough to harvest, and by that time more efficient means of moving logs to mills would be available.

CHAPTER SIX

1901-1923: RAILROADS AND FIRES

Sand Run and its immediate surroundings had slowly recovered during the 1890s, although signs of the logging and skidding and log floats would be visible for several more decades. Immediately following logging, and especially during heavy rains, silt flowed directly into the stream. But slowly it healed, and other than the presence of a few lodged logs that changed the currents and pools of Sand Run, aquatic life differed little from that prior to the log float.

Alders and viburnums, and even a few birches became established along the banks. Stump sprouts and seedlings gave promise that the forest would regenerate to fill the swath of barren land lying adjacent to Sand Run. Sunlight blanketed the ground and innumerable seeds germinated. Within five years a dense stand of young conifers bordered both sides of Sand Run. Ecological succession, that process by which barren ground is slowly replaced by a sequence of plant communities until a mature forest is present, was obviously underway. The horse logging that successfully moved logs to the banks of Sand Run had little impact on the fertile seedbed, and the sunlight and nutrients and rainfall worked together to produce a vegetative cover that would reduce, if not completely stop, soil erosion.

Healing of the waters and woods that had been so ravished by the logging and log floats was well underway by 1910. The riverbed and riverbanks showed no signs of log floats, other than the few logs that had been stranded and abandoned. The only evidence that a major event had taken place was the dense growth of seedlings and saplings that had become established in those areas where trees had been felled and skidded. Somewhat similar events had occurred throughout Canaan Valley prior to human encroachment, though always on a much smaller scale. Violent windstorms, limb-shattering ice storms, and devastating floods had flattened the forests, but only in relatively small patches. Those openings had quickly filled with new growth, and less than fifty years later it was difficult to identify the sites where major storm events had left their mark.

As cities along the eastern seaboard grew, the demand for

lumber continued. By 1900 it became evident to the lumbermen who operated the mills in Davis that they would soon run out of logs to saw into boards if they depended solely upon log floats to move logs to their mills. The logical response was to extend the railroad into the large tracts of standing timber surrounding Davis. Railroad spurs shot out of Davis. If viewed from high above, they resembled the spokes of a wheel as they slowly extended in all directions—west down both sides of Blackwater Canyon toward Hendricks, north along the North Fork of the Blackwater, east along Beaver Creek, and south toward Canaan Mountain.

None of the construction had any effect on Chelydra, who had confined both her summer feeding range and her winter hibernaculum to the lower end of Sand Run. Her home range covered two hundred yards of Sand Run, with the upper end of her range located near the former site of the beaver dam, the last hibernaculum for her mother. The first October following her move into Sand Run she felt the urge to hibernate, the same urge that would revisit her each autumn of her life. Snapping turtles are typically drawn upstream or up a side tributary to select their hibernacula. Chelydra explored two small side streams that flowed into Sand Run, but neither had the necessary combination of shelter and moving water essential for survival. Finally, one night during the third week of October she entered one of the larger tributaries flowing from the nearby hillside. Sixty yards upstream the tributary flowed through an alder thicket, and there Chelydra found the hibernaculum that would serve her well for over twenty years.

Chelydra had grown to eighteen pounds, with prominent features more characteristic of dinosaurs than of most modern-day reptiles. Especially conspicuous were the keel-like projections that jutted from the top of her shell and from the top of her tail. Their primary purpose was to provide protection against those few mammalian predators foolish enough to risk injury from the jaws of this powerful reptile. The hooked beak on both the upper and lower sharp-edged jaws accentuated the head, which had grown so large that it seemed out of proportion to the rest of the body. Muscular legs, armed with curved claws nearly one inch in length, added to Chelydra's imposing appearance.

The introduction of railroads, with their accompanying Shay engines and the newly-developed cable skidders, made it possible to cut most trees in Canaan Valley and haul them to the Davis mills. The railroad was extended up the Blackwater River to Camp 70 in 1915 and then across the Valley to Glade Run in 1916. At that point it was only two miles from Sand Run, and once again Chelydra experienced the impact of man's intrusion into her life. She never saw the heavy wood ties and the even heavier steel rails being laid along the east side of the Valley. But upon emerging from hibernation during April 1918 she heard and felt the driving of spikes as the railroad neared the big bend in Sand Run where the stream turned west after flowing north down the east side of Canaan Valley. Luckily for Chelydra, the stretch of Sand Run that constituted her primary home range was nearly one mile west of the railroad. As a result there was no direct threat from the railroad or the loggers or the cable skidders that transformed an awesome, pristine wilderness forest into a desolate wasteland.

Due to World War I, the high price of lumber made it economically feasible to extend the railroad to all cutover lands throughout Canaan Valley, and as a result no area was left untouched by the loggers. The tumult that had impacted the area near the towns of Cass and Spruce a few years earlier was now assailing Canaan Valley. Logging continued until 1922 when the last stands were felled and the last logs loaded onto railcars and hauled to Davis. Because areas along Sand Run logged during the 1880's were blanketed by young sapling stands, Chelydra was initially sheltered from any impacts of the second wave of logging.

Unfortunately for Chelydra and the other aquatic inhabitants of the lower end of Sand Run, the railroad track crossed directly over Sand Run in two places. The first sign that life in Sand Run was to be drastically altered was the silt and mud that swept down the stream during periods of heavy rain. But those events were minor compared to the life-threatening devastation that followed later that decade.

The stands of spruce and fir and hemlock that covered most of the floor of Canaan Valley during the 1800s had created a unique environment. Where the dense canopy had blocked out most of the sunlight, a cave-like atmosphere existed. Although conifers were evergreen they did drop their needles, but never all at one time. Because of the acidic nature of needles and the moist conditions that existed under the conifer stands, their needles did not rapidly decay as did the leaves of maples, birch, and black cherry that grew on the hillsides around Canaan Valley. The partially decayed layer of needles, branches, and other tree litter under the conifers had built up over the centuries until it was over two feet deep in many places. Thick beds of soft green moss covered that litter-layer and added to the moist, nearly optimum conditions that were so important to the complex community of amphibians.

But change, drastic change, began immediately after the first stand of trees was felled. The forest floor began to dry out as soon as the tree canopy was removed. The sunlight and wind sucked the moisture from the soil litter. In less than two years many of the wood frogs and toads had disappeared. The isolated ephemeral pools dried up earlier and earlier each spring and the wood frogs failed to reproduce. Soil invertebrates no longer provided the food essential to the survival of countless numbers of frogs, toads, and salamanders, as well as the shrews and ground-feeding songbirds. To keep their skins moist, some salamanders buried deep into the forest litter, but that was only a temporary solution—most died.

August of 1923 was extremely dry, with less than one-half inch of rain falling the entire month. By September the waters of Sand Run were so low that the resident fish and frogs and crayfish were forced to move to the few deep holes large enough to provide their needs. In contrast, some wildlife benefited from the drought. In addition to Chelydra, great blue herons, water snakes, and mink were attracted to the easy meals in the pools and applied extra stress to those animals seeking refuge there.

Chelydra felt the urge to hibernate during the second week of October, and after darkness had settled over the Valley she left Sand Run and moved up the tributary to the hibernaculum she had selected twenty years earlier. Lightning slashed through the sky as she slowly crawled up the slow-moving stream. She had witnessed lightning many times during her nighttime foraging, and felt no fear from the light spectaculars. However, this time was different and she had much to fear, although not from the lightning itself. This was a powerful, lengthy lightning storm that continued long after Chelydra had crawled under the old hemlock log half-submerged across the tributary. There she would stay for the next six months, in a barely conscious state.

The lightning reached the ground in many spots, and one particular strike targeted a dead spruce snag that had been left standing by the loggers. The top of the eighty-foot snag exploded, and pieces of bark and branches were flung from the dead tree. Most pieces fell into the super-dry duff of needles and branches that remained after the logging crews had pulled out of the area. Some pieces smoldered from the lightning strike, and in one spot fingers of smoke slowly curled up from the litter. The storm brought no rain to the Valley, and a small flickering flame later replaced the fingers of smoke. But no flame could remain small given the tremendous amount of fuel that covered the ground, and within minutes flames were rapidly spreading downwind. The fire had started in the upper end of Glade Run and with the winds blowing out of the northeast the flames moved south towards Sand Run.

This was not the first wild fire in Canaan Valley and certainly would not be the last. Sparks from Shay engines had started many fires during logging operations, but loggers had managed to extinguish most fires before they spread totally out of control. A few that were not extinguished burned over hundreds of acres, but those were restricted to the north end of the Valley where the railroad spurs had first been constructed.

The fires that erupted throughout Canaan Valley that night did not lack for fuel. In addition to the deep litter layer, an unbelievable number of hemlock logs that had been stripped of their bark and left to rot were scattered among the endless sea of stumps. A tannery had been built in Davis during 1886, and it required a continuous supply of hemlock bark to tan the hundreds of thousands of raw, salted beef hides shipped by railroad into Davis. Hemlock lumber had such low value that it was not worth the effort to move the logs from woods to mills. More than two hundred thousand hemlock logs, containing nearly seventy-five million board feet of lumber, were wasted to provide tanned leather for the shoes, coats, saddles, and other leather goods in such demand in eastern cities.

When the logs burned they produced a few ounces of ash to fertilize the soils of Canaan Valley. Logs that did not burn rotted slowly over the next thirty years, providing not only fertilizer for the plants that followed, but also protection for the myriad invertebrates that sought sanctuary beneath the organic shelters. Predators such as salamanders and shrews followed their prey under the logs, and in turn found food and shelter. Even without their outer layer of bark they played an important role in the recovery of the populations of invertebrates and small vertebrates that had once played such an essential role in the functioning of the Canaan Valley ecosystem.

Had the fires never spread and the seedbed remained intact, the forests would have rapidly regenerated and life would have returned to Canaan Valley. Conifer stands of red spruce, hemlock, and balsam fir would have once again covered the floor of the Valley. Maples and black cherry would have covered the hillsides. However, once the super-dry layer of needles and leaves was ignited, the flames rapidly spread up the Valley and deep into the soil. Where the litter layer was deepest, the fires smoldered for over twelve months; even the snows and rains of winter did not extinguish many of them.

The larger animals able to run or fly had abandoned the Valley as the railroads, and later the clearcutting, denuded their habitat. Because the logging was so widespread and took place over such a short period of time, the only refuges for the wildlife of Canaan Valley were along the banks of the Blackwater River and its tributaries where logging had taken place nearly thirty years earlier. The young stands of trees that had regenerated following the original logging of the 1880s provided temporary protection for many animals, including bobcats, northern flying squirrels, red squirrels, saw-whet owls, barred owls, goshawks, and northern waterthrush.

The fire spread that night from the tinder-dry forest duff into the many young conifer stands along Sand Run. The apparent refuges became deathtraps for animals that had sought shelter within their dense stands. Songbirds fled before the flames, but Cooper's hawks and goshawks were the primary beneficiaries of that wild flight. By the next day the fire had reached Sand Run and winds pushed the flames toward its headwaters and west into the dense stand of young spruce that bordered much of the lower end.

Small mammals, such as red-backed voles and masked shrews, tried to escape by retreating into the deepest ends of their burrows. But few survived, as the heat and smoke and lack of oxygen reached deep into the soil. Young spruce seedlings exploded into flames as the fire pushed toward Chelydra's hibernaculum. A forest fire draws enormous amounts of oxygen from the surroundings and the lack of oxygen killed many animals even before the smoke and flames reached them.

Although all of Chelydra's shell was underwater, her nostrils projected slightly above the water into a pocket of air immediately below the large spruce log. Had there been no drought the previous summer, and the small stream been at normal depth, the pocket under the log would have been completely filled with water. Chelydra felt the heat from the fire and instinctively drew her head deep under water. Although only semi-conscious, she dug deeper into the mud that prevented the flames and smoke from reaching under the hemlock log where she lay submerged. Luckily for her, the fire quickly passed over her hibernaculum and the temporary shortage of oxygen had no lasting effects.

Other fires had been ignited by that same lightning storm, and they were rapidly spreading across the North Branch and the Little Blackwater. Except for those aquatic species living in the Blackwater and other major streams, the wildlife of Canaan Valley were essentially wiped out by those fires and others that followed. Chelydra was one of the fortunate animals. However, she would not totally escape the impacts of the logging and subsequent fires.

The vast spaces of Canaan Valley that had been devastated through logging and fires had become nearly worthless to the lumber companies. But all parties did not deem the land valueless. In 1923 the West Virginia Power and Transmission Company (later to become known as Monongahela Power and then Allegheny Power System) purchased the large Marshall Tract, which covered over thirteen thousand acres in the north central end of Canaan Valley. Their plans were to construct a dam on the Blackwater River to supply water for a hydroelectric plant that would provide electricity to northern West Virginia.

The Power Company, for various reasons, did not proceed immediately with development of the power project. However, the implications of a lake that would inundate thousands of acres would hang over the Valley for nearly seventy-five years. Such a project would destroy most snapping turtle habitat within the Valley. Chelydra and other snapping turtles, along with the frogs, water snakes, kingfishers, great blue herons, mink, and raccoons found in and along the streams and rivers of Canaan Valley would be seriously impacted. The only unthreatened animals would be upland species such as squirrels, rabbits, bears, bob-cats, grouse, and turkey. All of the plant communities on the Valley floor would be eliminated, and only the hillside habitats would remain if such a lake were to be constructed.

CHAPTER SEVEN

1924-1925: POST-FIRE RECOVERY

The winds that drove the fires across Canaan Valley served also to eliminate the smoke that accompanied the flames. However, weeks after the main fires had run out of fuel and their flames flickered out, the litter layer continued to smolder. This produced clouds of lung-filling smoke, which hung over this natural bowl of a valley for weeks. A few fortunate individuals found refuge in the occasional isolated stands of spruce that were growing in widely-scattered bogs, but lethal smoke claimed many of those lives. It was many months before the winter rains and snows cleared the air to the point where wildlife breathed freely. By then there were few animals left in Canaan Valley to experience the relief.

The ashes that fell into Sand Run did little harm to Chelydra or the other aquatic life, and actually served as fertilizer for the wetland plants growing in and along the stream. With the loss of tree cover and the resultant loss of shade, water temperatures in Sand Run increased. Considerable silt washed into the creek and brought disastrous results to the crayfish and snails and fish so important to Chelydra.

Following the fires, silt and sunlight combined to create conditions so unhealthy that many aquatic species were eliminated from the stream system. The rains that followed the fires washed huge amounts of mud and muck, silt and organic matter into Sand Run. Sunlight striking Sand Run throughout the ten hours of daylight during October raised the water temperatures above sixty degrees. Silt suspended in the stream absorbed the heat from sunlight and increased the water temperatures even more. As water temperatures increased, amounts of dissolved oxygen decreased.

One inhabitant especially impacted was the brook trout, the most abundant gamefish throughout Sand Run and the rest of Canaan Valley. Brook trout, the only native species of trout that lived in Canaan Valley streams or the Blackwater River, needed cool water with high amounts of dissolved oxygen to survive and reproduce. Conditions in the cool, shaded waters of the Blackwater and its many tributaries had been nearly optimum for brook trout during the pre-logging era. Water temperatures rarely rose above sixty degrees, due to the shading effect of the dense canopy of conifers over most streams. Although darkly stained from the tannins, streams rarely carried any noticeable amounts of silt or sediment.

The brook trout in Sand Run were not quite as large as were those in the deeper sections of the Blackwater River, but they were just as colorful. Few individuals weighed more than two pounds, compared to some in the Blackwater that reached nearly four pounds. During early November, the trout heeded an urge as strong as the one that pulled Chelydra into her hibernaculum. The females searched out those stretches of Sand Run that had gravely or loose sandy bottoms and began to create shallow depressions by sweeping away loose material with their tails. By the middle of November numerous spawning beds, also known as redds, were scattered throughout the lower section of Sand Run. Males did not assist in the construction of redds, but they were not far away. The pinkish undersides and slightly hooked lower jaw distinguished the brilliantly colored males from the somewhat drabber females. The most prominent markings highlighted the lower fins, especially the pelvic and pectoral fins that had a milky white margin bordered by a black line. Only less striking were the small red spots, haloed with pale blue, scattered along their sides.

Courtship rituals culminated with the release of eggs by females and the follow-up fertilization by males. An occasional large female produced over three thousand eggs, but most released fewer than five hundred. Following fertilization, the females worked rapidly to brush the eggs down into the protective crevices of the gravel bed that would protect them during the coming months. Similar to most fish and other aquatic organisms, a super surplus of eggs was necessary to assure that a few young survived. Both male and female brook trout abandoned their redds shortly after eggs were deposited. Small minnows, crayfish, and numerous other aquatic invertebrates consumed large numbers of the eggs in the days that followed. Only those that managed to fall deep into the gravel developed into the young fry that hatched the following March.

In pre-fire years the gravel substrate of Sand Run had provided near perfect incubation conditions for brook trout eggs. Water temperatures remained below forty degrees and the highly oxygenated water flowed freely over and around the eggs all winter long. But conditions in Sand Run following the fires were drastically different from those of former years.

That year, the eggs dropped by the females were soon covered with silt. This greatly reduced the amount of oxygen that could be absorbed into the egg and subsequently most eggs failed to develop. Not one single egg hatched and not one trout fry was produced in the lower end of Sand Run that winter. In only one small pool of cool, clear water from an underground spring that flowed into a tributary of Sand Run were any trout fingerlings produced. This scenario was repeated throughout Canaan Valley. Only in those isolated pockets where silt was not a major problem did any fry emerge from their gravel nest the following spring. Those lucky few that did hatch faced an equally deadly threat.

Whereas hatching and development will not occur when water temperatures increase above forty-five degrees, the upper lethal limit for brook trout fry is sixty-four degrees. As the winter ice and snow melted away, the early spring sunshine was striking Sand Run in places that had never experienced direct sunlight in over one hundred years. By July, water temperatures of Sand Run had reached seventy-five degrees, too high above the critical temperature for any trout fingerlings to survive. The only adult trout to survive that terrible summer were those few that had found sites where upwellings of cold spring water kept water temperatures below the lethal level.

The conditions that were so detrimental to the brook trout population of Sand Run did not impact Chelydra as she quietly spent her winter dormancy unaware of the problems that would face her when she emerged from hibernation. Winter rains extinguished most of the deep fires that had smoldered until late November and the water that flowed over and around Chelydra contained much more silt than was normal. Although the amount of oxygen was much below what was optimum for a hibernating turtle it was adequate to supply her minimal needs and the following spring she would show no ill effects from the fires.

When Chelydra emerged from her hibernaculum in April she was greeted by silence. She heard no wood frogs or spring peepers, no woodcock or snipe, no mallards or black ducks, no saw-whet or barred owls. The sounds of wildlife should have dominated, but silence was the prominent feature that spring.

The near-absence of birds, whose presence was typically the most pronounced of all wildlife, created an eerie stillness. An occasional raven broadcast its throaty croak as it flew high above the Valley from Canaan Mountain to Cabin Mountain. The isolated calls of an occasional green frog that had survived in Sand

Run could not compare to the chorus that had been so characteristic of the landscape in previous years.

The powerful steam engines with their riveting whistles no longer rolled up and down the Valley; they, like the wildlife, were only a memory. When logging of the great Canaan forests was completed, the trains had slowly pulled up the train tracks behind them. The last trips out of the Valley brought not logs, but the great iron rails, ensuring that no trains would ever again rumble through Canaan Valley. The wooden ties and beds of gravel and rock and cinders remained, but in the distant future they would provide a foundation only for four-wheel drive and all-terrain vehicles. Those winds that had once begat blasts through the treetops produced only meek whispers over the blackened stumps. Never in the past millennium had such a large area (over one hundred thousand acres) experienced such a significant change in its landscape in such a short time. The Valley that had once been a vibrant living system was now a wasteland of barren hillsides and silent stumps. It appeared that life had been extinguished from this once-magnificent wilderness, but the land was not dead. Just as a desolate, winter woodland transforms itself into a vibrant spring scene overflowing with life, so would the blackened remains of Canaan Valley spring to life, though not quite so quickly.

When Chelydra vacated her hibernaculum in early April she faced a serious problem, how to find enough food to survive. Snapping turtles fed little during April and early May, but as soon as their body temperatures increased they consumed large amounts of whatever was available. By mid-May Chelydra was seriously hungry. The scarcity of food was quite perilous, and on many days she could not find enough to satisfy her hunger. Some days she was able to catch only one crayfish or one minnow, not nearly enough to satisfy the requirements of a twenty-pound turtle. Luckily for Chelydra, snapping turtles are not strictly carnivorous, or she could not have survived that summer.

One benefit of the increased sunlight that warmed the waters of Sand Run was an increased growth of aquatic plants. Pondweeds and rushes and sedges mysteriously appeared in many of the quiet pools throughout Sand Run. Although Chelydra much preferred meat to vegetation, she could not be choosy. Whereas in previous years she cruised the shoreline searching for crayfish or frogs or worms or fish, she spent her feeding hours that summer searching for the small beds of pondweed and other aquatic plants that would satisfy her hunger.

Chelydra survived the summer, but actually lost nearly one pound of body weight and entered hibernation with very little fat reserves. But she was lucky, compared to many animals that starved to death that summer. The warm, silted waters that flowed down Sand Run seriously harmed all fishes and many aquatic invertebrates. Animals that typically deposited their eggs in and around the gravely bottom produced few, if any, young during the next few years. Numbers of crayfish and snails and several species of minnows were greatly reduced as reproduction was nearly eliminated. Although there existed in West Virginia many species of invertebrates and fish that could survive in waters that were typically warm and silted, few of those were present in Sand Run at that time.

Brook trout are carnivores, as are most fish in cool, mountain streams, and they need an abundance of invertebrates to supply their food needs. The combination of warm water, decreased dissolved oxygen, heavy silt load, and scarcity of invertebrates was so serious that only in the upper reaches of Sand Run, Freeland Run, and Club Run, and in one spring-fed tributary of the Little Blackwater did brook trout survive. The logging and fires had almost eliminated those colorful native trout and they would be lucky to survive the ten years following the fires.

Some animal species did not survive. For a few species, every individual that had existed in Canaan Valley prior to the logging and subsequent fires was killed. Beaver were totally extirpated from Canaan Valley. A few survived the fires, but the lack of food resulted in their deaths or their dispersal out of Canaan Valley. Snowshoe hare and red squirrels, ruffed grouse and wild turkey, and almost all of the songbirds were forced to flee or die. For most, the forced evacuation resulted in their deaths. When the prey species disappeared from Canaan Valley, so did the predators—black bears and bobcats, river otter and fisher, barred owls and goshawks. Although most were mobile enough to relocate into surrounding areas, few survived the smoke, fire, stress, and starvation.

Whereas most terrestrial wildlife disappeared, a few aquatic predators remained. Mink numbers were greatly reduced, but a few found enough fish and frogs and crayfish to insure their survival. Those sleek glossy-brown members of the weasel family, that were such efficient hunters, persisted in the Blackwater River and in most of its major tributaries.

White-tailed deer were never abundant in Canaan Valley during the 1800s, the period when virgin forests of spruce, hemlock, fir, black cherry, and maple covered the land. By the turn of the century, following logging and fires, they were scarce in Canaan Valley and other parts of West Virginia. No more than one thousand deer were estimated to exist in West Virginia during 1910; the only survivors in Canaan Valley were in and around the headwaters of Little Blackwater River. Those few animals, probably no more than ten to twenty individuals, frequented the divide between the Little Blackwater and Stony River watersheds.

The early 1900s were a low-point in the history of wildlife of Canaan Valley. Not since the Ice Age of ten thousand years ago had wildlife numbers been lower. Although glaciers never extended into what is now called West Virginia, the conditions of the Ice Age limited the wildlife that could survive. But even when perpetual snow cover and never-ending winters prevailed over much of Canaan Valley, wildlife persisted.

Some species that had occurred in Canaan Valley during the 1700s did not survive through the 1800s. Elk and bison once roamed over much of West Virginia, with large herds being recorded along the Ohio and Kanawha valleys. These hoofed mammals provided an important food source for many settlers and by 1800 they had been almost eliminated from West Virginia. Canaan Valley was the site of the last recorded killing of an elk in West Virginia; three animals being shot by hunters in 1843. Only eighteen years earlier, around 1825, the last recorded killing of bison in West Virginia (a cow and her calf) occurred in Webster County. Bison were common in adjacent Randolph County and a few frequented the open glades of Canaan Valley and Dolly Sods.

Timber wolves, also known as gray wolves, did not survive long after the elimination of the large hoofed mammals. However, they were present in Canaan Valley prior to the arrival of the logging industry. When the first settlers arrived in West Virginia, these large predators had been fairly common due to the diverse prey base of elk, bison, and white-tailed deer. To provide protection for the sheep and cattle that were being raised on the many hill farms throughout the state, a bounty on wolves was paid from 1788 through 1900. In Randolph County, bounties were paid for fifty-six dead wolves in 1822 and for fifty-one in 1824. The last known wolf in West Virginia was killed in Randolph County in 1900.

Another wildlife species that was never again sighted in Canaan Valley after the arrival of the logging industry was the passenger pigeon. But the clear cutting of forests around Davis had no effect on those pigeons, the most abundant bird species ever to exist in North America. They were doomed long before Canaan Valley was logged and burned.

These colorful birds depended on huge amounts of mast—the fruits, nuts, and acorns produced throughout the hardwood forests of eastern North America. Market hunting, during which time passenger pigeons were slaughtered by the millions, coincided with the removal of large expanses of unbroken forests to cause the extinction of this magnificent bird. No bird species on earth has ever declined from superabundance to extinction in such a short period of time. The last flock known to occur in North America—estimated at 136 million birds—was sighted in Michigan in 1878 and the last known individual passenger pigeon died in the Cincinnati Zoo in 1914.

A few rare flocks (of "only" a few thousand pigeons) had visited Canaan Valley every fall during the early 1800s as the black cherry fruits and the beechnuts ripened. The Canaan mast crop, however, was not great enough to attract the large flocks of several million birds that John James Audubon reported from other regions of the eastern United States. Those trees that were most important to passenger pigeons, the oaks and chestnuts, were nearly nonexistent in Canaan Valley during the early 1800s when passenger pigeons were at their peak. Red spruce, balsam fir, and hemlock, the dominant tree cover of Canaan Valley, produced little, if any, mast that was preferred by passenger pigeons.

The conifer cover of Canaan did provide some benefit to those few flocks that visited. During late October, when the leaves had dropped from all the hardwoods, the birds temporarily crowded into the thick conifer branches to escape the cold winds blowing out of the north. Poorly equipped for survival in northern climates, the pigeons migrated to more southern states where they spent the winter consuming large quantities of not only hard mast, such as nuts and acorns, but soft mast such as wild grapes and viburnum fruits.

No herds of bison and elk, no packs of timber wolves, and no flocks of passenger pigeons would ever again visit Canaan Valley. But other wildlife would adapt to the new environment. During the next fifty years wildlife numbers would expand to levels exceeding those of the 1800s, or any previous century.

CHAPTER EIGHT

1926-1929: ECOLOGICAL SUCCESSION

Following another winter in her protective hibernaculum near Sand Run, Chelydra again emerged into a barren landscape. Although the silence of the previous year was occasionally broken by the breeding calls of a few green frogs, wildlife populations of Canaan Valley were little changed. While the fauna, the animal element, was still near an all-time low, the flora element had begun to recover. Chelydra, and the few other animals that populated that once-forested landscape, could not detect the unseen nearly miraculous changes that were taking place.

The great, blackened landscape had nearly disappeared. Only the many thousands of charred hemlock logs and charred stumps remained as evidence of the great fires that had so devastated the litter and limbs and young conifers along Sand Run. Rains had washed much of the blackened surface layer down into the remaining litter, and a few spruce seedlings had germinated in the wet areas bordering Sand Run. But the most significant promise of renewal was taking place out of sight beneath the sandy soils of the hillsides and the muck soils of the low-lying boggy areas. On every patch of ground with even the thinnest covering of soil, seeds were springing to life. The ashes, the rains, and the minerals all combined to create a seedbed that would nourish the resilient seeds that had survived the fires. Seeds are unbelievably durable and long-lived; some remaining viable for decades. Conifer seeds were most abundant along the low-lying areas with saturated soils, while hardwood seeds were most abundant on sandy hillsides. By removing the canopy and exposing soils to seeds, fires had created conditions conducive to the germination and growth of several plants that had previously been rare in the Valley.

Nature will not long tolerate emptiness; bare soil is wasteful. Plant life of some sort miraculously appears to initiate the progression of plants and plant communities that continue until the maximum possible biomass of plant life exists; in Canaan Valley this took the form of a mature forest of conifers and hardwoods. Life, or Nature as it is some times named, is resilient, not easily extinguished.

Dr. Maurice Brooks, arguably the greatest naturalist who ever tramped through the Appalachian bogs, wrote that, "Man despoils, but nature, given the opportunity, restores." By August, a greenish hue was visible to the ravens and turkey vultures soaring high over the Valley. Spruce, hemlock, and balsam fir seedlings were pushing out their soft green needles while less than one-inch tall.

Life would spring out of the formerly blackened earth like the fabled phoenix bird had sprung from the flames of fire. Mosses, both sphagnum and polytrichum, contributed to the dark green hue that gradually appeared. Lycopodium, also known as ground pine, was intermingled with the mosses. Ferns, both the low growing hay-scented and the nearly three-foot tall bracken, added to the plant life that would be widely scattered over the Valley floor by the end of the next growing season.

Ecological succession had begun. This phenomenal process by which a barren landscape is gradually transformed into a mature forest was definitely underway. The sequence of communities would predictably pass from a low-growing stage of mosses, herbs, and grasses, to a shrubby stage of blackberries, viburnums, St. Johns wort, and spiraea. Next to appear was a seedling-sapling stage of conifers, fire cherry, serviceberry, and aspen. That stage would eventually be replaced by a young forest of conifers in the lowlands and hardwoods on the uplands. Progress through these stages would be slow, but in fewer than one hundred years a mature forest would once again cover much of Canaan Valley. Although drastic and disturbing to humans, the logging and subsequent fires were insignificant in the sequence of events that had impacted Canaan Valley since its creation by geological forces nearly fifty million years ago.

Ecological succession is one of the few major ecological events that can be witnessed by humans during their relatively short lives. The life spans of most people are long enough that they can witness the progression of plant communities from barren areas to mature forests. Although the succession of animal communities is not so evident, it is just as predictable as is the sequence of plant communities. Certain animal species are present in the early stages, but as the vegetation changes they are replaced by other animal species.

Changes in bird populations are more noticeable to humans than are those of any other animals. In Canaan Valley, grassland birds such as swamp sparrows, bobolinks, and meadowlarks would be replaced by shrub species, such as gray catbirds, alder flycatchers, and common yellowthroats, and they in turn would be replaced by ovenbirds, rose-breasted grosbeaks, and indigo buntings, birds that preferred stands of young trees. In the final stages of succession, when mature forests dominated, pileated woodpeckers, barred owls, red-eyed vireos, and black-throated green warblers would be most prominent.

Changes similar to those throughout the various plant communities would occur in the populations of salamanders and mammals. But because of their secretive behavior, those changes would be much less obvious to humans. Neither the changes in plant communities nor those in animal communities were obvious to Chelydra or the other animals that inhabited Sand Run, the Blackwater River, or the other Canaan Valley tributaries. It would be nearly twenty years before the plants growing along

Sand Run would be established enough to impact the riparian zone animals living in that band of land bordering streams and rivers.

By May, the waters of Sand Run had moderated enough that Chelydra was quite active in her nightly activities of feeding and exploring. She had so expanded her home range that it stretched from the mouth of Sand Run to the bend where the stream flowed north-south, rather than east-west like the lower reaches. That one-mile stretch supported a diversity and abundance of food sufficient to provide the nutritional needs of a twenty-pound turtle, which Chelydra was.

During late May, Chelydra—now a fully mature turtle—felt a new urge as the waters warmed and her seasonal activities reached their peak. This feeling was different from anything she had ever experienced before. While she had hungered for the sweet flesh of fish earlier in May, she now longed for something else—but she knew not what. Unknown to Chelydra she had reached sexual maturity and the urge to mate had arrived. She would likely have reached sexual maturity several years earlier, but the shortage of food and the other drastic events that she survived delayed this key event in her life. Another key factor, the lack of male turtles, may have also delayed the event. This was so important that it would determine her success in passing on her genes to a new generation of snapping turtles. Chelydra wandered throughout Sand Run during the last two weeks of May, without really knowing why.

It was not food she desired, because she found enough minnows and crayfish and snails to satisfy her hunger. It was a mate that she unknowingly sought, but just as she did not know what she searched for, she did not know there were no male turtles in Sand Run. Actually, no other snapping turtles of either sex existed in Sand Run. Chelydra was the only turtle that had survived the predators, log floats, fires, and food shortages. A few other snapping turtles had survived in each major stream of the Valley, but those were widely scattered. There would be no successful reproduction until a male snapping turtle wandered into that section of stream inhabited by a female snapping turtle. But the same urge that visited Chelydra was being felt by all the mature male snapping turtles in Canaan Valley, and the once-a-year event would result in several cross-country excursions by those males. Hopefully, for the continuation of Chelydra's lineage and the future of snapping turtles in Canaan Valley, one or more male turtles would eventually encounter a female during the breeding season and a nest of fertile eggs would result. But no male snapping turtle would enter Sand Run that year.

The year 1928 passed uneventfully for Chelydra, except for one small incident in late August. Due to the lack of shade, water temperatures had risen above seventy degrees and the female turtle spent most of her time in the few deep pools scattered along Sand Run. One summer night as the moon was slowly rising over Cabin Mountain, Chelydra ventured out from her daytime retreat under an old hemlock stump that perched at the edge of Sand Run. Her feeding was greatly reduced, compared to that of April and May, and she did not feed every day. That night her senses detected the odor of a wounded minnow, one of her favorite foods. She slowly moved upstream in the direction of the minnow but her nose detected the odor of another inhabitant of Sand Run, a northern water snake. Those snakes were only slightly more abundant in Sand Run than were snapping turtles, and Chelydra had not encountered one during her nighttime forays of the past two years. However, she did retain faint memories of the one she encountered when only one year old, the one that had nearly made a meal of her. This was not the same snake, since that one had long ago been killed by a raccoon. Water snakes, and all snakes that lived in Canaan Valley, had a much shorter life span than did snapping turtles. Fifteen years was old for a water snake.

The snake was an adult female who had only the previous day given birth, twenty-three baby snakes each about eight inches long. Water snakes were but one of nine snake species in West Virginia that did not lay eggs; others were the garter snake, ribbon snake, queen snake, redbelly snake, brown snake, earth snake, rattlesnake, and copperhead. During mid-May the female had mated with one of the few male water snakes in Sand Run and had moved downstream from a small tributary a mile away to give birth to young. Embryonic water snakes complete their five-month development within the body of the female and are born encased in a membranous sack, much like the placenta of mammals.

Similar to snapping turtles, young snakes are precocial and receive no care from their mothers. Their survival depends on inherited skills plus a measure of luck. Most of the twenty-three baby snakes born to this particular female would be captured and eaten before they were one year old, thus providing food for raccoons, mink, and great blue herons.

The adult snake was in the act of swallowing a recently captured creek chub. Her needle-like teeth firmly held the small fish while her jaws maneuvered it toward her stomach. Once firmly in the grasp of her sharp teeth and strong jaws, few prey were able to escape. Chelydra had been lucky to escape her only previous close encounter with a water snake; two of her sisters had not been so lucky.

Fully-grown and over thirty inches long, the heavy-bodied snake blended into the shoreline due to her dark gray back and the reddish-brown blotches that patterned her sides. But Chelydra did not need to see the snake to pinpoint its exact location. Her sense of smell was much more useful than was her sense of sight, especially at night. She had hoped to enjoy a meal of fish, and the snake did not detect her presence until Chelydra was only twenty inches away. The minnow odor had triggered her appetite and a meal of water snake would be almost as satisfying as one of fish. The turtle made a quick lunge toward the snake and her six-inch neck suddenly thrust forward. Her sharp, powerful jaws closed over the head and neck of the water snake, which violently whipped its body around in the water. Other small fish quickly swam upstream away from the commotion and the sand and silt that were stirred up by the two struggling reptiles. Even if the head and jaws of the water snake had been free to strike the turtle, its teeth would have done no damage. The turtle closed her small eyes to prevent injury and the exposed portions of her head and legs were much too armored to be damaged.

Chelydra began to tear at the snake's body with her long claws while she bit deeper through the head and neck. In a short time the head separated from the body, which continued to twist violently on the bottom of the pool. Chelydra quickly swallowed the head and then completed her meal by consuming the remainder of the snake's body. That unusually large meal lasted her for several weeks and she ate only three more times before entering hibernation in October.

CHAPTER NINE

1930-1940: FARMING AND RESTOCKING DEER/BEAVER

Winter's snow and ice were slow to melt during 1930 and spring arrived later than usual in Canaan Valley. Chelydra did not emerge from her hibernaculum until the second week of April and, as usual, her first goal was to find a shallow pool of quiet water where the sun's rays would slowly raise her body temperature. Her temperature had stayed near thirty-five degrees during hibernation and she would not eat until her body temperature was above sixty degrees.

Signs of spring were scarce that year, just as they had been for the three previous years. A few spring peepers were heard along the shallows of Sand Run, but the sounds of breeding birds were rare. Other sounds drifted across the Valley floor that month, but they were not the sounds usually associated with a remote mountainous region. Chelydra felt the loud booms as much as she heard them. They came from the upper stretches of Glade Run, only one-half mile north of Sand Run. Chelydra had experienced similar booms nearly forty-five years ago, when dynamite had been used to release the water from splash dams that initiated the great log floats from Sand Run to the sawmills at Davis.

The dynamite blasts felt by Chelydra that morning were produced by three men who were clearing blackened stumps from the hillside along the great middle ridge that formed the western border of Glade Run. One man was busy setting small charges of dynamite under the larger stumps in an attempt to blast them out of the ground. After he had successfully loosened five of the stumps one of the other two men led forward a team of large draft horses. The third man looped one end of a large logging chain around a blasted stump and fastened the other end to the double-tree on the harnesses of the powerful horses. The men guided as the horses dragged the stump down toward Glade Run where it was added to a small pile of stumps that they had removed the previous day. Many of the stumps were pulled directly from the ground by the team of horses, and dynamite was needed only for the larger stumps that were deeply rooted.

The men could clear only twenty to twenty-five stumps in a day, but by May they had cleared an area of nearly ten acres. When the soil was warm enough and dry enough, they used a plow pulled by the same team of horses to turn the dark earth. The humus and litter on the hillside had not burned as deeply as had the deep layer under the dense stands of conifers in the soggy soil along Glade Run. Adequate fertile sandy soil still existed and their efforts produced a promising looking field ready to be planted.

The technique used by the three men and those who had cleared land in other sections of Canaan Valley was quite similar to that used during previous centuries. Native Americans and early settlers had used the same method to cultivate the flat, fertile river bottoms and the gently sloping hillsides throughout West Virginia. Settlers had cut trees, using the logs for houses and barns, and then burned the remaining tops and branches. Using horses and dynamite, they removed stumps and then plowed the fields to grow corn, oats, wheat, flax, and vegetables they so desperately needed to survive.

Native Americans had used similar practices for hundreds of years to grow their corn, beans, and squash. It took them longer to completely clear a field, because they had to burn out the stumps, but they still succeeded in growing enough crops to survive. Canaan Valley was the last area in West Virginia to have land cleared for farms. Nearly all river bottoms and hillsides in other regions of the State had been cleared by the late 1800s. No Native Americans ever cleared land or established permanent camps in Canaan Valley, due to the uninviting climate and the thick, forbidding stands of conifers that covered much of the Valley.

Settlers in other forested areas of West Virginia had been able to clear only two or three acres per summer and required at least three summers to clear land for their homesteads. Most of their time had been spent felling trees, usually with an axe, and moving the logs for the construction of log cabins and barns. Because of the prior logging and subsequent fires settlers in much of Canaan Valley did not have to spend time felling trees. They were able to clear enough land in only one summer to begin farming. However, they did have one major problem. Unlike pioneers who had settled in forested areas, those in the northern end of Canaan Valley had few logs for houses, barns, or fences. Ironically, they were in the region that had produced the greatest amount of lumber of any region in West Virginia, but there was little lumber available for their buildings in 1930.

The same trains that had shipped carloads of lumber out of Canaan Valley were used to ship lumber back to Davis ten years later. Much of the building material came from other sections of West Virginia, but some came from western Maryland. After the lumber arrived in Davis it was loaded onto long wagons drawn by teams of horses to the homestead sites throughout the Valley. The railroad beds that remained following the removal of rails provided access into the Valley. With many of the wooden ties intact, travel, at best, was a bumpy trip, but it certainly beat trying to haul heavy wagons through the great expanse of stumps and bogs that would have proven to be serious obstacles. The railroad grade that followed the Blackwater River into the northern end of the Valley was the main route taken by those settlers who were clearing farms along the middle ridge. They needed to ford the Blackwater River, but that was easy during the summer months.

More than two dozen different farms were cleared in the Valley between 1900 and 1925. Most were concentrated in the southern end where more suitable uplands were available. Only three farms were located in the northern end of the Valley. All sites to be cleared for farms were markedly similar. They were upland locations that had formerly grown hardwoods rather than conifers. They were gently rolling, free of large rock formations, and contained springs that flowed year-round. Such springs were common along the middle ridge and lower hillsides of surrounding mountainsides, but the settlers took extra care to assure the spring's dependability even during the driest months.

The farm being cleared along Glade Run was situated beside just such a valuable spring, and one of the first tasks was to clean and enlarge the opening in the earth from which it flowed. Stones were used to form the base of a springhouse, and a small building was constructed over the spring to keep out animals as well as any debris that might be blown in.

A logging camp had originally been built at the Glade Run site and a small field had been cleared to grow hay for the teams of horses that were so essential to hauling logs. A bunkhouse and a small barn for the horses and their hay had been erected during 1921, and were used by the settlers who hoped to farm the hillside.

All farms in Canaan Valley aimed to be self-sufficient, thus they needed cultivated fields for crops, pastureland for livestock, plus hayfields where the grasses could be harvested. Life was hard on every hill farm that had ever been cleared in West Virginia, making it nearly impossible to be totally self-sufficient. But life on the newly-cleared farms in the northern end of Canaan Valley was even more challenging. The scarcity of trees resulting from logging and fires was a major problem. Stumps and stones were dragged from the cleared fields to build fences around vegetable gardens and cornfields. If a farmer wanted to fence in a larger field, however, it was necessary to bring in fence posts by horse-drawn wagons. To be self-sufficient in Canaan Valley, a farmer needed sheep for meat and wool, cattle for milk and meat, chickens for meat and eggs, and horses to pull wagons, plows, and mowing machines. Livestock were left free to forage during much of the year, but when the deep snows of winter covered the ground there had to be adequate hay to prevent their starvation. That required cutting and then curing grasses in the pear-shaped, conical haystacks that were so efficient in shedding rain.

One reason the specific farm site along Glade Run was selected was because of the fields of blue-joint grass scattered along the lowlands. The stream was named for the large areas of the surrounding land that were open glades, covered with a variety of natural grasses. Such fields, or glades, provided forage during summer months, in addition to the all-important grasses that were harvested for hay.

Unlike the early settlers in other parts of West Virginia, those in Canaan Valley could not depend on hunting and trapping to provide meat. This same region had once supported deer, elk, and bison, in addition to an abundance of brook trout. Those food sources, however, no longer existed in Canaan Valley and the settlers had to grow all the food they needed to raise a family.

Another chapter in the history of Canaan Valley was underway. The farming era would last somewhat longer than the logging era, but would generate much less income for the region. Compared to the logging era, it would have only a minor impact on Chelydra and the other aquatic animals of Sand Run. The farm family that settled along Glade Run never saw Chelydra, although they did occasionally explore the upper reaches of Glade Run and nearby Sand Run.

Once again the mating season for snapping turtles came and went, with no males showing up in Sand Run. It would be another unproductive year for Chelydra and for most turtles in Canaan Valley. There was, however, successful reproduction of many prey species in Sand Run. Although waters were too warm to support brook trout, the creek chubs successfully spawned and produced a crop of fingerlings that would eventually provide food for Chelydra. Crayfish and snails released their fertile eggs as did the few green frogs that frequented the grassy banks of Sand Run.

Green frogs were the largest frog living in Canaan Valley, measuring nearly four inches from snout to rump; their outstretched legs extended another four inches. The back of a green frog was greenish brown, while the sides of the head below the eye were green. The frogs spent most of their time sitting along the bank and Chelydra was lucky enough to be within striking distance of several that jumped too close to her jaws. Frogs were a welcome food, along with the minnows and crayfish that provided most of the meat in her diet.

Green frogs emerged from hibernation in the muddy bottom

of Sand Run at almost the same time as did Chelydra; the emergence of both species was triggered by the same warming waters. Temperatures in April were much too cool for the green frogs along Sand Run to begin calling, but by the second week of May their two or three note, banjo-like calls could be heard all along Sand Run.

Several of the female green frogs living alongside Chelydra deposited their egg masses in late May. Each egg mass was nearly one foot in diameter and contained several thousand eggs. The eggs hatched in six or seven days, but the tadpoles did not transform into frogs until the following summer. They wintered in the same mud as the adults and had grown to slightly more than one inch in length when they finally developed their legs and lost their tails. Because the tadpoles were small and remained hidden along the edges of streams, they were rarely eaten by Chelydra. However, the tadpoles did provide meals for other predators and by the time they changed from tadpoles to froglets fewer than one hundred had survived from each large egg mass.

By 1930, much of the Valley was supporting some type of vegetative cover. There were many areas, however, where only dark soil and even darker stumps could be seen. This was especially true where the dense stands of conifers had stood. Mountainsides had sprung to life with stands of red maple, sugar maple, fire cherry, and black cherry. Scattered pockets of red spruce and balsam fir were present along Sand Run and Glade Run, but these were scraggly compared to the nearly five feet tall red maples. Stands of aspen were nearly six feet tall and were present along all the major waterways. Grasses and shrubs were also established and well on their way to forming dense thickets.

The near-phenomenal recovery of plant communities throughout much of Canaan Valley had not passed unnoticed by the West Virginia Conservation Commission (now the Department of Natural Resources, WVDNR). Although vegetation was well established, many of the animals that had been residents during the early 1800s were noticeably absent. No one expected to see bison or elk grazing across the Valley floor, but they were disappointed that no white-tailed deer were present. Adequate food resources were available, but there were too few deer in surrounding areas to naturally repopulate Canaan.

Deer remained nearly nonexistent throughout much of West Virginia, increasing only slightly from a low of about one thousand animals in the year 1900. Restricted hunting and habitat regrowth following logging had enabled deer in most regions of the State to recover slightly, but numbers ranged from low to absent. Responding to numerous requests, biologists from the West Virginia Conservation Commission released eighty-nine deer into eleven West Virginia counties during 1921-1930. Most were obtained from Michigan, and eight were released into Canaan Valley. An additional seventeen were released in Canaan Valley during the 1930s.

The regrowth of tree cover along watersheds throughout most of West Virginia produced adequate habitat for many animals whose numbers had been so drastically reduced that they were nearly eliminated. Most species were able to repopulate all of their former range with no assistance, but others were unable to do so. Beaver had been totally eliminated not only from Canaan Valley but from all counties in West Virginia by 1920. Surveys by Conservation Commission biologists during the early 1930s indicated that Canaan Valley was capable of supporting a population of beaver. Adequate food supplies, in the form of aspen stands and alder thickets, were available.

The Conservation Commission, aided by the U.S. Forest Service and sportsmen's groups, released sixty-four beaver into nine West Virginia counties during 1933-1940. Six of these were released into Canaan Valley in 1936, and four were released at Lindy Run along the lower Blackwater River in 1935. The beaver were purchased from Michigan and Wisconsin, where populations had recovered following the devastating fur trade of the 1800s.

A few other wildlife species would be reintroduced into Canaan Valley by the WVDNR in later years, but most wildlife recovered naturally, just as did the plant communities. The mosaic of habitat types that became established in the 1930s would eventually support a much greater diversity and abundance of wildlife than had ever occurred in Canaan Valley. However, the plant communities that would unfold would be greatly altered by deer and beaver, with some plant species nearly eliminated and others greatly reduced. Next to humans, no other animals would have such a significant impact on the Canaan Valley ecosystem.

CHAPTER TEN

1941-1944: GAS WELLS

Emerging from hibernation, Chelydra began another rather uneventful April. As sunshine slowly raised water temperatures, the turtle increased her daily activities. Although it had started as a typical year, this one would be drastically different from any other the mature turtle had experienced. Late one night, as a quarter-moon appeared above Cabin Mountain, she detected an unusual odor floating with the current down Sand Run. It had been over thirty years since she last experienced the odor, and she had difficulty identifying it. Though curious about its source, she remained in her normal home range that night. The next night the odor was even stronger, and although she still had not identified it, she was attracted to it. As she approached the upstream limits of her home range, where Sand Run turned south, the odor became so strong that she knew the source was not far away. Drawn toward it, she slowly realized that it was another snapping turtle; the first one she had encountered since the last of the snapping turtles had been killed by log floats and fires. Although attracted and curious, she did not know why. Snapping turtles are not territorial and she had no inclination to defend the stretch of Sand Run that she called home.

The two turtles came close enough that they could see and recognize each other as a snapping turtle, even though the quarter-moon contributed little to visibility. They approached and sniffed shells. Chelydra did not realize it, but the sex of this visitor was extremely important. Was it a male or female?

Chelydra was getting old; except for humans she was the oldest living animal in Canaan Valley. At fifty-six years of age she had long ago surpassed the other "old" animals of the Valley. The oldest black bear that occasionally ventured into the Valley had lived twenty-five years, half the age of Chelydra. One deer had lived twenty years before her death indirectly caused by missing teeth. Some of the mid-sized animals, such as foxes, bobcats, hawks, owls, and turkeys had reached ten years of age before dying. Smaller animals had life spans that rarely exceeded two years; typically the smaller the animal the shorter time it lived.

Snapping turtles, because they were larger, lived longer than any other reptile or amphibian in Canaan Valley. But they also managed to live longer than the larger mammals, primarily because turtles had an extremely low metabolic rate. The act of hibernating six months out of every twelve seemed to translate into a doubling of their life span. By essentially going into cold storage, with all body processes nearly stopping during the six months of hibernation, aging was temporarily halted.

Although Chelydra was the oldest living animal in the Valley, she was approaching the end of life and had never produced offspring. Her specific combination of genes, which had been so essential in providing her with the skills and instincts to survive, were in danger of disappearing forever. None of her sisters and no other hatchlings from any eggs laid by her mother had survived. Other turtles in Canaan Valley had been only slightly more successful. During the late 1920s, in both Freeland Run and Mill Run, a male and a female turtle had managed to find one another and nests of viable eggs had been produced. Snapping turtle populations were on their way to recovery, but it would be several decades before these reptiles were present in all the waterways of Canaan Valley. Fortunately, males wandered long distances when they had streams and wetlands to follow.

The newcomer to Sand Run was a male who had lived in the lower end of Glade Run. He had unsuccessfully searched the entire upper half of Glade Run for a female that spring, but had found none. Moving overland during an all-night rain, he eventually reached a small tributary of Sand Run. Although not as old as Chelydra, the male had mated in previous years with a female that lived in the lower reaches of Glade Run. After nearly an hour of close inspection, Chelydra moved away from the male. She was feeling two urges, and hunger was the stronger of the two. After consuming two crayfish and a green frog, she returned to her retreat under the roots of a yellow birch where she remained that night and all the next day. The male moved a short distance downstream and located another cavity under the bank where he remained all of the next day.

The two turtles left their retreats as the last light of dusk disappeared and they cautiously swam toward each other. Although not exactly friendly, the two turtles remained close to one another during the next three hours. During the time of complete darkness when only the stars provided the briefest of light, the male turtle approached Chelydra from behind on several occasions, but she always moved off. Finally, nearly five hours after sunset as the quarter moon appeared over Cabin Mountain she did not move away and the male swam up behind her. Using his claws to grasp, he climbed atop Chelydra's shell. His weight pushed her onto the bottom, but because she was in shallow water his head and the upper part of his shell remained above water.

The somewhat smaller male was able to grasp her shell tightly with his four feet, while Chelydra instinctively twisted her tail around to the side. The male turtle curved his tail down beneath her shell and inserted his extruded penis into her cloaca. The turtles remained coupled for nearly twenty minutes, during which time the male emitted low-frequency, deep-throated bellows that radiated over fifty yards up and down Sand Run. Those mating sounds mingled with the calls of night birds and frogs and the trickling of Sand Run as it flowed over and around the many rocks characteristic of that stretch.

The two turtles finally separated, moved apart, and began searching for food. The same mating behavior was repeated the following night, after which time the male moved up Sand Run toward Glade Run. Chelydra resumed her normal activities, but the changes taking place within her body were something she had never before experienced. The sperm from the male had fertilized twenty-seven eggs.

In late June, nearly thirty days after mating, Chelydra felt one of the strongest urges she had ever experienced. As a warm rain fell over the Valley, the turtle crawled out of Sand Run and began slowly moving away from the stream. Although she did not have a specific destination in mind, she was instinctively drawn to a spot barren of any vegetation, and elevated somewhat above the water level in Sand Run.

The female turtle had moved over sixty yards from Sand Run when she located a small, elevated, sandy mound. After two intense hours of uninterrupted digging the hole was deep enough, and eggs began to slowly fill the bottom. When all twenty-seven eggs were deposited, she filled the hole with the displaced sand and headed back toward Sand Run. The success of the clutch of eggs would depend upon soil temperature and moisture, along with being undetected by predators. Chelydra's clutch was lucky. June rains soon washed away all odors left at the nest site and none of the raccoons and skunks living along Sand Run stumbled upon the eggs.

Chelydra felt indifferent at having deposited her first clutch of fertilized eggs and resumed her normal summer-time behavior. One night in late July her routine was altered. Water levels had dropped significantly due to low rainfall, and the riffles of Sand

Run became quite shallow. Chelydra moved somewhat awkwardly and cautiously as she walked across the riffle; a move from one pool to another was usually not dangerous. That particular riffle was nearly thirty feet long and when about half way across Chelydra noticed a large dark animal moving in front of her. The animal approached closer and the turtle turned and tried to hurry back to the pool she had just left. But turtles can not hurry when walking. They might walk somewhat faster than normal, but compared to most animals they are exceedingly slow. The animal saw Chelydra and circled while sniffing cautiously in her direction.

It was a yearling black bear, weighing nearly 140 pounds. An adult bear would have avoided the turtle, realizing that the threat of a severe bite far outweighed the slim possibility of a meal. But this was a yearling male that had never before encountered a snapping turtle and had more courage than sense. The bear slapped at the turtle with its front paw several times during which time the turtle pulled her head and legs back into the shell. Chelydra snapped at the bear but never caught the paw that continued to slap. During one swipe the bear's claws slipped under the edge of the turtle shell and the female was quickly flipped onto her back. Chelydra immediately extended her long neck and pushed herself back upright. The bear seemed to think this was a game and again tried to flip Chelydra, but his paw moved in front of the turtle rather than along her side. Her head and neck suddenly thrust forward and the knife-sharp jaws closed around the bear's foot. The young bear squalled in pain as the jaws cut deeper. Blood spurted from the bear's foot and Chelydra clamped down harder.

During the fight, if it could be called that, the bear was jumping and dragging the thirty-eight pound turtle. After realizing that he could not pull his foot loose the bear clawed at Chelydra with his other foot and also attempted to bite her shell. Finally the bear pulled his foot partially out of Chelydra's mouth, leaving two toes clamped between her jaws. The jaw muscles of the turtle contracted again and the two toes were removed as cleanly as if a meat clever had severed them. The bear ran wildly down Sand Run, splashing and bawling in pain, while Chelydra swallowed the two toes.

Chelydra had not escaped unharmed. The bear's claws had slashed open one of her hind legs and one of the bear's canine teeth had punctured her neck. Turtle blood mixed with bear blood on the rocks of the shallow riffle that night.

The injured turtle slowly crawled back across the riffle into the pool and then into a deep burrow that had been the bank den abandoned several decades ago by the last beaver family in Sand Run. The burrow extended deep into the bank and because of the protection it provided, muskrat, mink, and turtles had used the burrow on many occasions. Chelydra was hurt, although the injuries did not appear to be fatal. Increased water temperatures of late summer caused snapping turtle activity to decline and Chelydra often went several weeks without feeding during August. Injuries received during the bear encounter caused her to be even more immobile, and she remained in the den for over two weeks, while the wounds began to heal.

Chelydra did not hear the sounds of the small bulldozer as it moved down the hill toward Sand Run, although there was considerable clanging and banging. A narrow road was being cleared the length of the middle ridge to accommodate the drilling rigs that were being brought into the Valley. Gas wells were planned for several locations in Canaan, three of which would be on the middle ridge. Upon reaching Sand Run the bulldozer began pushing dirt and rocks over the edge of the bank to create the footer for a small bridge. After completing work on the south bank the dozer drove across Sand Run and began working along the north bank. Unfortunately for Chelydra, the den where she was recovering was at the exact location where the bridge was to be built.

A truck with large pipe arrived two days later. Because of her injury, Chelydra had made no attempt to flee from the opening. She heard the rocks and dirt cover the mouth of the burrow, but did not immediately realize the danger. After darkness settled in she attempted to swim out, but several feet of rocks and dirt blocked her way. Finding no openings, she retreated deep into the burrow. Soon after the truck with pipe had arrived, a crew began erecting the pipe foundation for the bridge. Thick-walled, twelve-inch pipes were driven into the ground, while similar sections were welded together to form the frame to which heavy timbers were later added.

Small amounts of fresh air filtered into the burrow, but barely enough to satisfy the minimum needs of the turtle. Because she was in a state of semi-hibernation, her metabolic rate slowed and she required much less oxygen than she would have needed in April or May. Had the bulldozer arrived in May, and Chelydra not been injured by the bear, she would have dug frantically to escape. Unaware of the danger, she made no further attempts to dig out from her eventual tomb. The bridge was completed by late August and drilling rigs and truckloads of workers drove across the bridge and onto the northern end of the middle ridge.

Wild animals do not fear death; they are not even aware of the meaning of life and death. They use every means possible to survive, but not because they know that the alternative is to die. Chelydra did not panic, and although her injuries did not heal, they caused her little pain. As the oxygen supply slowly diminished, she entered deeper and deeper into a state similar to hibernation. Had the temperatures in the burrow been lower she might have survived through winter. Her heart stopped beating the first week of October. Violent death caused by the claws and teeth of a predator or the hands of humans would have been much quicker, but not more merciful. Her death could have been much worse.

Thus the life of the fifty-six year old turtle came to an end. She had witnessed the apparent destruction of the Canaan Valley ecosystem, but had also been present during the recovery when it became obvious that the devastation caused by logging and fires was not irreversible. She had been an onlooker as beaver, deer, turkey, and a host of other wildlife had disappeared. However, as life returned she had also been a functional part of a unique ecosystem. There were other snapping turtles scattered throughout Canaan Valley, and there was a clutch of Chelydra's eggs buried along Sand Run that contained twenty-seven embryonic turtles carrying Chelydra's genes. Populations of this all-important reptile would increase, although slowly, and the role it played in maintaining the balance of the ecosystem would become ever more important.

CHAPTER ELEVEN

1945-1960: CAULIFLOWER PRODUCTION AND DEER HUNTS

The following spring, Chelydra's one and only clutch of fertile eggs lay safely buried in the sandy soil nearly two hundred yards upstream from the new pipe bridge over Sand Run. Ground temperatures during the previous summer, when the embryos were developing, had averaged sixty-eight degrees, and as a result all embryos had developed into females. Shortly after the last of winter's snow and ice had melted away and adult turtles were emerging from their hibernacula, the first baby turtle pushed its head up through the sandy soil. Twenty-two more baby turtles followed and all instinctively headed for Sand Run. No raccoons or ravens saw the hatchlings as they tumbled over the bank into the small stream, and there were more turtles in Sand Run that April, although all were but hatchlings, than there had been in over fifty years.

Chelydra had been a good mother; as good as a snapping turtle mother could be. Although she had not lived to see any of her offspring, she had given them a strong start in life. She had selected an excellent site to lay her eggs, she had given them a combination of genes that would result in the survival of an unusually large number, and she had secured her clutch.

In addition to the emergence of several new clutches of turtle hatchlings, other important developments were taking place in Canaan Valley that spring. Farmers in the southern end of the Valley were experimenting with a new crop. Over two thousand acres of land had been cleared in the southern end, most of which were devoted to growing hay and raising cattle and sheep. Although farmers had tried to grow corn, they soon learned that the short growing season made it impossible for the ears to mature. However, the cool, moist climate made Canaan Valley nearly ideal for the production of another crop. Scientists from West Virginia University had determined that cauliflower could be successfully grown as a cash crop in Canaan Valley.

Cauliflower was first planted on a commercial scale in 1944, when five farmers planted seven acres. The operation was quite successful that year, and farmers realized a net return of nearly six hundred dollars per acre. Commercial production increased steadily until 1954 when forty farmers planted approximately eighty acres. However, it became evident that future success of this cash crop was seriously jeopardized by two problems: damage by deer and poor growth form. Deer had exploded to unbelievable numbers by 1950, and farmers soon learned that they must build six feet tall fences around their fields to protect the cauliflower. The second problem was not so easily solved. Buttoning (the development of small unmarketable heads) destroyed almost half of the crop in 1954 and nearly 90 percent in 1955. The financial hardships created by constructing deer-proof fences, combined with the two crop failures, forced many farmers to abandon efforts to commercially grow cauliflower. Thus, the commercial production of a cash crop came to an end and no other cash crop would ever again be raised in Canaan Valley.

Chelonia, the first of the female turtles to emerge from the nest, was the first of Chelydra's offspring to reach Sand Run. She instinctively sought shelter beneath the overhanging bank and watched as her sisters spread out among the rocks and roots bordering the stream. The next six months would be the most critical of their entire lives and only nine of them would survive to enter hibernation. Raccoons, mink, water snakes, and great blue herons would take a heavy toll on the hatchlings, plus a few would succumb to accidents and starvation.

Throughout Canaan Valley, crops were being produced by Nature—crops of seeds and fruits, leaves and grass, beaver and bobcats, deer and turtles. And just as the crops of cauliflower were harvested, so were the crops of Nature. These crops were harvested not by humans, but by wildlife: plants by herbivores, and they in turn by carnivores. Chelonia soon learned about the worms, crayfish, snails, and tadpoles that provided the nourishment she needed to survive. And just as importantly, she learned to avoid the numerous predators that were such a threat to helpless little turtles. The instincts of her mother and all her ancestors had been passed on to guide Chelonia. These instincts along with lots of luck combined to assure her survival that summer.

Sand Run supported a surplus of easily obtained food for Chelonia and her sisters, but it also supported many other animals. A two-year old male beaver had left the Blackwater River in May and selected Sand Run as the location of his first dam. The site was east of the middle ridge and nearly three hundred yards upstream from the stretch frequented by Chelonia. Stands of aspen and alder covered much of the floodplain in that area and provided more than enough food for several beavers. Young beaver live with their parents during their first two years, but then are forced out to make room for the new litter. The parents of this youngster were two of the adult beaver that had been released by the WVDNR nearly ten years earlier. This young male had been forced out of his family's home territory in April and had wandered up and down the Blackwater River until he was attracted to Sand Run. During the two years he spent with his family he had learned what foods to eat and how to build a den and a dam. That experience enabled him to construct a dam capable of impounding water, although it was probably not sufficiently strong to withstand an unusually large flood.

Most territorial mammals mark the boundaries of their territories, the defended area, by leaving scent at strategic places along the boundaries. The young male beaver had created several scent stations, consisting of small piles of mud and sticks along the bank on both sides of the beaver pond. To those mud piles he regularly added a secretion, named castoreum. While the main purpose of the scent station was to warn away other males, it also served to announce his presence to any young females that might venture near.

One night in early September, when the yearling male was starting to cut aspen trees from the nearby hillside to build his food cache, a young female detected his scent as she investigated the lower reaches of Sand Run. The three-year old female had lost her mate to a mountain lion that summer, and was wandering up and down the Blackwater River in search of an unmated male. It was the young male's good fortune that she decided to explore Sand Run that September night. The odor from his scent station told the female that a solitary male inhabited the site. If the male had a mate, her scent would have also been deposited at the scent station.

Because beaver are such social animals, and because both beaver needed a mate to survive, it was a matter of only five days before the two had reached an agreement. She was welcomed into the young male's bank den and the two shared the chores of repairing the dam and building the food cache, chores that were essential to their survival during the coming winter months. The dam was nearly seven feet tall at the downstream side and had a concave form; curving upstream into the pond. This provided the architectural strength of an arch, with the water pressure forces transferred to the ends of the dam where it was anchored into the bank. The two beaver also cooperated in digging canals that extended from the pond toward the nearby stands of aspen. Much of the mud removed from these canals was carried in the beavers' front paws to the dam where it was used to plug leaks.

Numbers of deer in Canaan Valley had grown to incredible numbers during the twenty years following their reintroduction. Near-optimum deer habitat covered much of Canaan Valley and there were no major predators. An occasional black bear or bobcat accidentally stumbled across a newly born fawn, providing a quick meal for the lucky predator. But black bear and bobcats were not capable of killing full-grown deer. Actually, they could not even catch fawns once they had reached two weeks of age. The only predator capable of catching full-grown deer was a mountain lion, or cougar. An occasional mountain lion wandered into the Valley from the adjoining wilderness of Dolly Sods and usually killed one or two deer before returning to the preferred seclusion of the mountaintop.

The Canaan Valley deer herd had grown to over one thousand animals by 1945, and over three hundred bucks were harvested by hunters that fall. The Conservation Commission realized that deer numbers were so high that agricultural crops and native vegetation were being impacted. To reduce deer numbers, a hunter-choice season was initiated in 1950. Hunters could legally shoot any sex and any age deer. Nearly one thousand deer were harvested in Canaan Valley during the 1950 fall hunting season, followed by a harvest of over three thousand deer during 1951. As a result, deer numbers were reduced to levels where there was little damage to agricultural crops or native vegetation. Deer numbers remained low for several years and fewer than one hundred deer were harvested in 1956.

Although the high deer numbers had no direct impact on Chelonia, they did indirectly impact many animals along Sand Run. Deer are plant eaters, grazing on herbaceous plants during summer and browsing on woody plants during winter. During winter, when snow concealed grasses and other herbaceous plants, deer were forced to feed on those plant parts that protruded above the snow. The only available browse were the low-hanging branches of trees or the ends of seedlings that barely reached out of the snow. Most tree seedlings were so short that they were buried by snow during their first year. But during their second and third years their tops were within easy reach of deer.

The most serious impact of the overpopulation of deer was the drastic alteration of plant communities. Deer eliminated or greatly reduced regeneration of many plants due to repeated feeding. The most noticeable of these were the balsam fir, hemlock, and hawthorne. Succession during the 1930s had progressed along a predictable route and at a predictable rate. During that period of low deer numbers, trees grew above the reach of deer. However, few young fir, hemlock, or hawthornes survived once deer numbers reached levels beyond the biological carrying capacity of Canaan Valley. This term is critical to understanding the health of an ecosystem, and refers to the number of healthy animals that can be supported on a given unit of land, without adversely affecting other plants or animals.

While deer reduced numbers of balsam fir and hemlock, the conifer stands so important to many animals in Canaan Valley were not seriously impacted. It was fortunate that deer did not eat red spruce, except as a starvation food. Young spruce seedlings were able to grow and mature and produce more seedlings, while the balsam fir and hemlock that died of old age or disease or storms were unable to replace their own species.

Aspen was another plant that was heavily browsed by deer during winter. Both trembling and big-tooth aspen grew rapidly, but not fast enough to escape severe browsing by deer. Beaver numbers are more dependent upon aspen than upon any other tree; the more aspen stands, the more beaver colonies. And, the more beaver colonies, the more beaver ponds. And, the more beaver ponds, the more snapping turtles. When Chelonia emerged from hibernation the spring after the two beavers built their dam, the newly created pond became the center of her home range. The beaver increased the size of their den and dam that spring, to provide more space for the two kits that were born in April.

Beaver and snapping turtles got along fairly well, with little interaction. A full-grown snapping turtle is capable of capturing a young beaver, but they rarely have the opportunity to do so. Young beaver do not venture out of the den until June or July, and by that time they are too large for a snapping turtle to attack. But beaver indirectly benefit snapping turtles in several ways. Turtles seek shelter in abandoned dens and lodges during summer and hibernate in the beaver dams during winter. Although Chelonia did not use abandoned dens or lodges and did not hibernate in the beaver dam, she did benefit from the deep waters of the beaver pond. The warm waters around the edge of the pond provided an endless bounty of worms, snails, crayfish, minnows, and tadpoles.

There were dangers in the beaver pond, even more than along

Sand Run. The abundance of prey species attracted a never-ending parade of predators. Luckily for Chelonia there were no adult snapping turtles in the area, but a mink lived near the pond and several large water snakes moved into the pond the year after it was built. A great-blue heron visited the pond each day and raccoons explored the shoreline each night.

Obviously, Chelonia would benefit from the food and shelter provided by the beaver pond, but her young life would be constantly at risk of predation. Stands of grasses and sedges had appeared in the shallow waters along the edges and provided cover for Chelonia and five of her sisters who also resided in the beaver pond. The escape cover provided shelter for them to feed safely while hidden from view. Hiding places where Chelonia could avoid detection were much more abundant in the beaver pond than among the shallows of Sand Run.

Because food was a greater attraction than was the threat of predation, Chelonia remained in the beaver pond. Precocial animals, those required to survive without any direct assistance from their mother, respond more to positive attractions such as food than to negative features such as predators. The act of catching and consuming a tasty minnow provides positive reinforcement to stay at that site and try to catch another. But the act of being caught and eaten by a mink teaches nothing. A dead animal does not learn to avoid the predator that took its life.

The two beaver in Sand Run and all the beaver in Canaan Valley were being harmed by deer overbrowsing the aspen. Beaver and aspen have a unique symbiotic relationship, one in which both species benefit from the presence of the other. Although symbiotic relationships are not common in nature, they do exist in many ecosystems. But, the aspen-beaver relationship is one of the very few involving a tree species and a mammal. Beaver can and do eat a wide variety of both woody and herbaceous plants. But beaver populations reach their greatest densities where there are extensive stands of aspen.

Beaver easily cut down the soft-wooded aspen trees and the nutritious bark, which is the only part of the tree eaten, is easily removed and digested. Aspen trees grow in dense monoculture stands, usually containing no other tree species. Due to the dense shading from the canopy of aspen branches, no young aspen seedlings grow under the stand. When aspen trees die of old age, usually thirty to forty years, there are no young aspen trees, or any other types of trees, to replace them. However, if a healthy aspen tree is cut down before it reaches old age, hundreds and even thousands of young aspens grow up from the roots. These root shoots, as they are called, grow quickly because they use the still-living roots of the parent tree for transporting water and nutrients. Clear-cutting of an aspen stand by beaver will produce a new stand of aspen within a few years. In contrast, the natural death of a stand of aspen due to old age will typically result in that stand being replaced by other tree species—species that are, unfortunately, not nearly so nutritious for beaver.

CHAPTER TWELVE

1961-1969: WOODCOCK SURVEYS AND BEAVER ECOLOGY

The sights and sounds of spring once again greeted Chelonia when she crawled from under the log where she had spent the last six months of hibernation. She slowly made her way down the small tributary to Sand Run and moved into the shallow end of the beaver pond. The engineering skills of the two beaver had produced a dam that was able to withstand the flood waters resulting from the spring rains and the pond was slightly larger than it had been the previous year.

The beaver family numbered six: two adults, two yearlings from the previous year, and two kits. Mating had taken place in early January and following a gestation period of 128 days the female had given birth in early May. Born fully furred, the two kits entered life with their eyes open and within a few days were moving around inside the den.

Chelonia saw the adult beaver and their two yearlings every night as they left the den to feed and do maintenance work on the dam. But she did not see the two kits until late June when they finally made their first exploratory trips outside the den. The young beaver were easily kept afloat by their dense fur coats and they quickly learned to dog paddle around the pond. They continued to nurse throughout June, but slowly began to nibble on the succulent vegetation that grew in the warm waters of the pond. The young beaver and the young snapping turtles often swam near one another as they both cruised the shoreline in search of food. The small turtles were certainly no threat to the beaver, and the beaver, being strictly vegetarian, were no threat to Chelonia or her sisters.

Young turtles and young beaver grew in size that summer, but whereas the growth of the beaver kits was quite noticeable that of the young turtles was not nearly so. By October, the beaver kits had gained more than ten pounds while the turtles did not gain even one pound. Beaver required only four years to reach their full weight of fifty pounds, whereas the turtles required at least thirty-five years to reach a weight of forty pounds.

The beaver pond that had been created by the beaver family increased in size during the next six years. Chelonia and her two surviving sisters grew to nearly three pounds and several new litters of beaver kits were born in that Sand Run bank den. But Chelonia never saw more than eight beaver swimming around the pond at any time. The two-year old beaver were always forced from the pond by the parents during late spring, to be replaced by the kits that were born that same spring. One year there had been four kits, but the usual number was two.

As the beaver pond increased in size, conditions became even more suitable for Chelonia. More aquatic vegetation became established and her prey base expanded greatly. Invertebrates were so numerous that Chelonia never had to search long for a meal. Vertebrates also increased in numbers and added significantly to the healthy functioning of the beaver pond community. A pair of muskrats had moved into the pond as beds of succulent plants became established and mink and raccoon paid nightly visits to its perimeter. Great-blue herons and green-backed herons were daily visitors, while other birds had built their nests in the vegetation that formed a distinct border around the pond.

The most prominent of these were the red-winged blackbirds, especially the males. The females' feathers were quite dull, in contrast to the brightly colored males, with their red shoulder patches glistening against the background of shiny black feathers. As with most songbirds, the males had bright colors to advertise their presence and mark their territories, while the females had dull colors to remain inconspicuous.

Song sparrows, swamp sparrows, and yellowthroats all

nested in the spiraea, goldenrod, and sedges that bordered the pond. An American bittern had built her nest in a dense stand of marsh plants and a mallard had constructed her nest in dense grasses on the adjoining hillside.

Amphibians and reptiles had also been attracted to the beaver pond and added to the biodiversity of the community. In addition to the water snakes, green frogs, American toads, and spring peepers, there were salamanders. While the snakes were potential predators, the amphibians were potential prey. Chelonia had eaten numerous tadpoles and salamander larvae during her first few years of life, but she was too small to attack one of the larger amphibians. At age ten, however, a salamander swam slowly past her as she lay quietly along the edge of the beaver pond and Chelonia instinctively grabbed at the easy meal, clamping her jaws around the midsection. Instead of enjoying the delicious flavor of a minnow or a frog, she experienced a burning, irritating sensation. The animal she had grabbed was a red-spotted newt, and its toxic skin secretions made it unpalatable to Chelonia and most other predators. Chelonia dropped the squirming salamander in less than one minute and learned that no matter how easy they were to capture, newts should not be eaten.

The greenish-brown salamander was characterized by scattered black dots and small, black-bordered red spots along each side. Its belly was yellow with numerous, small, black spots. One of the most prominent features was its strongly flattened tail that was used to propel it through the water. In addition to the aquatic form that Chelonia had attempted to eat, this species had a distinct terrestrial form, known as a red eft. Whereas the aquatic form (newt) had rather smooth skin, the terrestrial form (eft) had rough granular skin.

The newt that Chelonia had caught was a female. She had laid nearly three hundred eggs during early May, attaching them singly to stems and leaves of submerged plants. Her eggs had hatched within three weeks, and the larvae transformed into the red eft stage by late summer. The hatchling efts left Sand Run and moved into the nearby forest, where they would remain for up to seven years. After that, the efts would return to the beaver pond and then transform into the aquatic newt stage.

Although the waters of Sand Run were still too warm to support brook trout, numerous creek chubs were present in the beaver pond and the stream flowing into it. The great diversity of wildlife that inhabited the beaver pond was a result of the beaver transforming a flowing stream into a quiet pool. In so doing, they created conditions that were suitable for dozens of other animals. Beaver are the only animal, other than humans, that create a totally new environment for their own use.

Chelonia survived the many predators that frequented Sand Run and grew to nearly twelve pounds during the next three years. She was the only turtle in the pond. A raccoon had eaten two of her sisters and the others had moved farther up Sand Run. August 1964 witnessed another significant event in the life of the twenty-year old turtle. Whereas she typically encountered several beaver while cruising the shoreline looking for crayfish or frogs, that week in August was different. There were no beaver in the pond; they had totally abandoned their home of ten years. Typical of most beaver colonies they had run out of food. Beaver rarely travel farther than three hundred feet from their pond to cut aspen. The effort required to haul the branches and sections of logs back to the pond becomes too great at those distances and the danger of predation increases.

Towards the end of summer the adult beaver had concluded there was not enough aspen on the surrounding hillsides to fill the food cache essential for survival during the coming winter. The adult male made several exploratory journeys both upstream and downstream of the dam and determined that over thirty acres of nearly mature aspen were present about one-half mile upstream. After returning to the den, he communicated to the other members that they should follow him to their new home. The entire family, two adults, three yearlings, and three young-of-the-year, immediately began building a bank den, a dam, and a food cache. While watching their elders repair the dam that summer, the youngsters had learned enough to be of considerable assistance. Although they could not haul large tree sections, the small branches they could haul were essential in sealing the dam and the bank lodge. The food cache, nearly ten feet wide and thirty feet long, was completed by early November. Although several early-season snowfalls had occurred, the pond had not frozen over and the beaver were able to work throughout the nights. Their fur coats had thickened in preparation for the cold weather that would soon arrive, and the snow and cold water did not slow their efforts. With a food cache, a bank lodge, and a one-acre pond that was nearly six feet deep, they were well prepared for the next five months of winter.

Chelonia was aware that the beaver had abandoned their old pond, but she was not aware of the consequences. Shortly after the beaver had gone, she left the pond and moved up a nearby tributary until she reached her hibernaculum of previous years. There were only minor changes in the beaver pond that winter as water levels dropped six inches due to small leaks. The construction skills of the beaver had produced a dam that survived the winter rains without their assistance. The dam did not, however, resist the heavy runoff following two days of rain in late March, and a small portion of the dam washed away. Water levels had dropped nearly two feet by the time Chelonia left her hibernaculum and returned to the pool in mid-April.

The abandoned beaver pond was only three feet deep, but still provided adequate water for crayfish, minnows, frogs, and other important prey. She had no reason to leave and spent that entire summer in the pond. But changes were taking place. As water levels dropped, the exposed mud created an excellent seedbed and new growth of marsh plants covered the barren flats by August. Red-winged blackbirds, swamp sparrows, and song sparrows still nested around the pond, while raccoons and mink regularly visited the pond in search of a meal. By early October, the abandoned pond looked quite different from the pond of a year earlier, though it was still recognizable as a beaver pond. Without beaver to make the needed repairs, the leftover dam would continue to fail with each heavy rain, causing the dam to give way little by little.

When Chelonia returned to the beaver pond the following spring, only a small, quarter-acre pool of water welcomed her. The spring floods had caused serious damage to the dam. The small pool, in conjunction with the natural pools situated below the dam, provided barely enough deep water for Chelonia. She remained in the area that summer, although in her nightly forays she ventured much farther up and down Sand Run than before.

While Chelonia and the other inhabitants of the beaver pond adjusted to their new environment, a significant change was occurring at the site of the abandoned pond. Just as ecological succession had created a productive plant community following the fires, succession began to create a productive plant community within the boundaries of the abandoned beaver pond. This progression would occur much faster than did that following the fires. Silt washing down Sand Run had accumulated on the bottom of the beaver pond. The resulting layer was quite fertile, with rich, saturated soils covered by plants before summer's end. Beaver had thus indirectly created a second community; this one was a beaver meadow.

The newly created plant community was of little value to Chelonia and the other aquatic animals of the original beaver pond. But, just as different plants became established, so would different animals inhabit the grassy meadow. As the aspen stands on the nearby hillsides were rejuvenating, a rejuvenation of the beaver pond was taking place. This new habitat type would add to the mosaic of communities that characterized the Canaan Valley ecosystem.

May was an exciting month for the wildlife of the Sand Run watershed. Most animals were intimately involved with some facet of reproduction and all were driven to renew the body reserves that had been depleted during the stressful winter months. The nightly onset of darkness prompted Sand Run's nocturnal animals to initiate their nighttime activities. Chelonia was acquainted with each of the Sand Run animals, but an unfamiliar intruder appeared that night.

While the turtle began her evening feeding forays, a bright light flashed across the beaver meadow. The light lingered a few minutes, then moved over the nearby fields. About fifteen minutes later the light swept over her again, this time concentrating on the grassy area along the edge of the beaver meadow. Although Chelonia and other nearby animals were aware of the light, they did not alter their normal nighttime behavior. Moonlight and lightning often penetrated the darkness, but the light that night was much more powerful than any natural light Chelonia had experienced.

As Chelonia paused at the edge of the small pool of water that was a remnant of the once-larger beaver pond, a figure became visible. It was a man, and he carried a three-foot wide net attached to a six-foot long handle. The man moved cautiously onto the grassy area, being careful to avoid the direct beam of the spotlight. He paused, then suddenly dropped the net onto the ground. Running forward, he dropped onto his knees and carefully grasped something that was fluttering under the net. His experienced hands reached beneath the netting and slowly removed a small, brown bird with a bill nearly three inches long. The bird was a woodcock, and the man was a wildlife biologist.

Woodcock, or American woodcock as they were termed in bird books, were one of those species that benefited from the early stages of succession. Whereas few, if any, woodcock existed in Canaan Valley prior to logging and fires, the intermingled aspen stands and grassy areas provided nearly optimum habitat for this member of the shorebird family. The favorite food of woodcock is earth worms, and the aspen and alder thickets that had sprung up around Canaan Valley during the 1940's supported prodigious amounts of those nutritious worms. Woodcock use their long bills to probe into the soft ground in search of worms and other invertebrates. When the sensitive tip of the woodcock's beak detects a worm, the flexible end opens and firmly grasps the prey. After carefully pulling it from the ground the bird swallows it whole.

The accumulation of decaying aspen leaves and alder leaves created ideal conditions for earthworms, and subsequently created ideal conditions for woodcock. The cover produced by vertical stems and horizontal branches provided excellent protection from any predator that might approach from the ground or the air.

An in-depth study of woodcock in Canaan Valley had been initiated by wildlife biologists from the WVDNR in 1964. Assisted by Wildlife Management students from West Virginia University, they were attempting to determine how many woodcock nested in the Valley and what areas were most preferred for feeding, mating, nesting, and brood-rearing. To determine population numbers they captured and banded the birds. Spotlighting was one of the most productive methods of safely capturing woodcock. One of the key areas they sampled regularly was the Sand Run drainage. After capturing a woodcock, the biologists determined its sex and then attached a numbered aluminum band around one leg before releasing it unharmed. The bird's sex was easily determined by measuring the length of the bill; if longer than two and five-eighths inches the bird was a female. Female woodcock are larger than males, most likely for sheltering the eggs and young during cold rainy periods so typical of Canaan Valley and other northern areas where woodcock breed.

The biologists captured six woodcock in the Sand Run watershed that night before moving up the Valley to Glade Run where they were able to capture seven more. Earlier in the night they had used another type of net to capture woodcock: a mist net. Those nets were stretched between poles and positioned to intercept males as they engaged in their nightly singing-ground flights. Upon returning to Canaan Valley each spring, as early as March, the males selected their individual singing grounds. There they performed the courtship rituals that attracted receptive females within hearing distance. To perform the ritual that consisted of two parts, males selected open areas characterized by bare ground and low-growing vegetation. During the ground phase, the males strutted around with their tail feathers spread wide and their wings stretched down almost to the ground. The aerial phase involved flights in large circles two hundred feet above the ground. The key to attracting the females was not the strutting on the ground or the spiraling flights overhead, but the calls. The courtship ritual occurred only at night, and it was necessary that the female hear the male because she could not see him until quite close. While on the ground he produced a series of nasal peents and while in the air he emitted several melodic warbling notes. Males engaged in this courtship behavior immediately after dusk settled over the Valley and often displayed for less than one hour. On nights with a full moon, however, they continued their courtship long into the night.

From previous night's observations, the biologists had determined the locations of several singing grounds and the best sites to erect their mist nets. After carefully removing a bird from the net, which was six feet high and twenty feet long, it was banded and then sexed; the majority of birds captured in mist nets were males. Males were captured when they took off or when they landed at the singing grounds, while females were netted as they flew in to mate with the males.

Female woodcock were also captured with the use of dogs. Female woodcock do not build a nest, but lay three or four buff-colored eggs with brown spots in a small depression among the leaves. Searches with dogs were conducted when females were on the nest or raising their young. Newly hatched woodcock are precocial, fully developed with eyes open, body covered with feathers, and legs capable of walking or running. They cannot fly when born, but in only two weeks they are capable of short flight. However, they cannot survive without a mother to provide shelter against the low temperatures and cold, spring rains. In addition, the mother teaches them to find worms that provide the protein they must have and introduces them to thickets that provide the best protection against Coopers hawks and sharp-shinned hawks that would greatly enjoy a meal of young woodcock. Birds such as woodcock, grouse, turkey, ducks, and geese are only partially precocial. In contrast, most amphibians and reptiles, including snapping turtles, are completely precocial. Those that survive do so with no direct assistance from either parent.

To locate and capture broods of woodcock, it was necessary that the dog be a pointer, one that would immediately freeze in position upon detecting the scent of a woodcock. English setters were the most preferred breed. A biologist would release his dog into an alder thicket or an aspen thicket and then follow closely behind as the setter cruised back and forth in search of bird scent. Most biologists attached small bells to their dog's collar so that their movements could be easily followed. A biologist would be warned as soon as the tinkling of the bell stopped and the dog went on point. The biologist then hurried forward and carefully dropped the long-handled net over the female and/or her young.

Wildlife biologists were successful in capturing and banding nearly five hundred woodcock in Canaan Valley during 1965 and 1966. That study continued for several more years, and several thousand birds were eventually banded in an attempt to better manage the populations of this fascinating bird that is such an integral part of the Valley ecosystem.

CHAPTER THIRTEEN

1970-1975: DAVIS POWER PROJECT AND CANADA GEESE

The 1970s witnessed several key events that would determine the future of the thirty-six thousand-acre watershed that defined Canaan Valley. Although most of the events would not change the face of the Valley as much as logging or fires, one had the potential to cause even more drastic changes. The panorama of the

1970s would bring more permanent and extensive changes than had either logging or fires. It is likely that Canaan Valley could have recovered from the devastation of logging and fires—had there been no human intervention. That scenario was of course impossible. Given several hundred years, the great conifer forests of red spruce and balsam fir would have once again blanketed the low-lying portions of Canaan. Obviously humans did intervene; removing large predators, farming the uplands, and contributing to the increase of deer and beaver. Unfortunately, the characteristics that made Canaan Valley so unique would contribute to its degradation. Interest in outdoor recreation carried a heavy weight.

Based on changes that had taken place in other areas of the United States, it should have been relatively easy to predict the future of Canaan Valley. There were only a few unknowns to be resolved, but they were monumental. The greatest potential impact involved the construction of a hydroelectric project. In 1970, Monongahela Power Company and its parent, Allegheny Power System, applied to the Federal Power Commission for a permit to construct the Davis Power Project. The company had purchased over fifteen thousand acres in 1923 for the purpose of eventually constructing a hydroelectric project along the Blackwater River, but for various reasons and for many years, the project was delayed. Initially, they had planned to construct a dam in Blackwater Canyon, downstream of Blackwater Falls. Studies indicated, however, that water flows during summer months were inadequate for the planned hydroelectric plant in the Canyon. Because their lands in the Blackwater Canyon were deemed unsuitable for power production, Monongahela Power deeded 446 acres to the

State of West Virginia in 1937, followed by an additional 935 acres in 1953. The State later obtained 744 adjoining acres from the U.S. Forest Service, and Blackwater Falls State Park came into existence.

The key component of the proposed power project was a seven thousand-acre lake, a facet that would have had an enormous impact on Chelonia, the other snapping turtles, and most aquatic animals throughout the Valley. Few species would have been able to live in the Power Company lake.

If Monongahela Power had applied for a permit in the 1950s or even the early 1960s, there would have been few, if any, delays in being granted the license. With the advent of NEPA (National Environmental Policy Act), however, and several new environmental laws and regulations, it would prove much more difficult to gain approval for the license.

The hydroelectric project would have directly impacted over eight thousand acres, one-fifth of the total watershed. While much of the remaining twenty-eight thousand acres was destined for change, such a large lake would cause widespread change both abruptly and intensely. Development had been occurring throughout the Valley since land was first cleared for the farms in the early 1900s. Farmhouses and barns, churches and schools, roads and gas wells, and a few stores had appeared throughout the Valley during the early part of the century. But in 1970, the northern two-thirds of the Valley contained no permanent structures, other than a few gas wells and a couple hunting camps. Even the southern third of the Valley presented a rural landscape, with widely scattered structures.

Chelonia and the other wildlife of the northern two-thirds of the Valley were not impacted by the development, because it had been concentrated in the southern end, avoiding the waterways and wetlands. The largest single project was the construction of Canaan Valley State Park. In 1957, the 3,135-acre Kaemmerling farm was donated to the State of West Virginia. During the 1960s, additional acreage around the Kaemmerling farm was purchased until the State owned six thousand acres. The ski lodge and several ski slopes situated along the southeastern corner of the Valley were opened in 1971. The golf course opened in 1972 and the main lodge was opened to the public in 1977.

While the possibility of the Davis Power Project was potentially the most significant event to occur in 1970, one other event would have a more immediate impact on Chelonia and other wetland wildlife in the Valley. When Chelonia returned to Sand Run during April 1970, after spending the winter in hibernation, she witnessed a bird that she had never before seen. While swimming along the shoreline of the abandoned beaver pond she encountered a large, black and white and gray bird. The bird was swimming back and forth along the shore and was much larger than any bird she had ever seen in Sand Run. Although not so tall as a great-blue heron, the bird weighed over ten pounds. The most striking features were the long, black neck and the white chin patch. While wary of the bird as a potential predator, Chelonia soon noted that its behavior identified it as a harmless neighbor. The bird was a Canada goose.

The bird was one of several released by the WVDNR in 1969 and 1970 in an attempt to establish a resident, breeding population in Canaan Valley. Canada geese regularly passed over the Valley during their annual fall and spring migrations from their wintering grounds along the Atlantic coast to the breeding grounds in Canada. But Chelonia was in hibernation when these birds passed over. A few had stopped for a rest on the Sand Run beaver ponds during previous years, but Chelonia was never aware of their brief visit.

The goose that Chelonia discovered was a male, also known as a gander. Two days later a second goose appeared in the small pond. The two birds were nearly the same size and so identical in appearance that Chelonia could not distinguish between the two. Later that week she noticed one of the geese sitting on top of the abandoned beaver lodge. Unbeknownst to Chelonia the goose, a female, was sitting on a clutch of four eggs. The bird swimming in the water was her mate. The two birds had arrived in Canaan Valley during the first week of March while snow still covered most of the ground and the quiet pools of Sand Run were covered with a thin layer of ice. Having spent the winter in North Carolina, the pair was eager to begin nesting.

The female had chosen the top of the abandoned beaver lodge for her nest, and after scrapping out a small depression, lined it with down feathers from her breast. Many days during April were sunny and quite pleasant for the brooding female, but during some nights, snow accumulated on her back from late-season snowstorms. Her down feathers were great insulation, and the breast feathers, coupled with her body temperature, maintained the eggs at the nearly-constant ninety-nine degrees that was so essential for embryo development.

Several times each day the female goose left the nest after using her bill to cover the eggs with a warm layer of down feathers. She remained off the nest only long enough to eat some of the green shoots growing along the pond before anxiously returning to the eggs. The male remained on guard a short distance from the nest to detect and drive away any potential predator that might approach. It was necessary for the gander to protect not only the female but also the eggs during the thirty-day incubation period.

Several predators regularly explored the shoreline along Sand Run in search of a nightly meal. One night a large male mink had approached the female and another night a small red fox stalked close in an attempt to jump on the female. In both situations the gander quickly responded and drove away both animals with wicked blows from his powerful wings. The site chosen for the nest was not ideal, and was very difficult to defend. The optimum site would have been on a small island or a beaver lodge surrounded by water. Both of the geese were three years old and, unfortunately, were inexperienced in selecting a nest site.

The large bobcat picked up the pleasant goose odor when nearly fifty yards upstream of the nest. He began his stealthy stalk through the tall grass, approaching to within thirty feet before the nesting female detected his movements. She immediately began honking loudly and the gander rushed toward the intruder. If the nest had been surrounded by deep water so the bobcat was forced to swim, the gander could have easily driven it away. The cat realized he had an easy meal. He had to dodge a few blows from the gander, but in one sudden charge he grabbed the female around the long neck and hauled her into the nearby bushes. The gander made no attempt to follow and remained near the nest all night. His honking did not stop until daylight appeared over Cabin Mountain, and he viewed the damage that had been done.

Feathers were scattered around the nest and one egg had been rolled over the side and lay partially submerged in the water.

Male geese do not share in the incubation duties while eggs are developing, and the gander felt no inclination to resume the duties of his now-dead mate. He walked around the nest and seemed to study the eggs, but then he returned to the stream where he spent the remainder of the day. Canada geese typically mate for life and he would not have an opportunity to find a new partner until he joined flocks of geese on the wintering grounds.

That afternoon a raven spotted the disturbed goose nest while flying over the Valley. The large, white eggs caught his attention, and he quickly flew down and alighted near the beaver lodge. He cautiously walked around the lodge, cocking his head from one side to the other, before concluding that he had nothing to fear. Hopping up to the nest he immediately began pecking at one of the eggs. The powerful black beak soon opened a hole in the shell and yellow yolk oozed out. Without hesitation, the raven began eating the yolk and pecking an even larger hole in the shell. The female goose had incubated the eggs for nearly three weeks and the embryonic goslings were well developed. After the raven had completely opened the egg he pulled out the partially developed gosling and quickly tore it into small pieces, eagerly devouring them.

The raven opened one more egg and ate much of the yolk. But rather than eating the unborn gosling, he grasped it in his beak and flew back toward Cabin Mountain. Flying directly to his nest he presented the prize to his mate who was sitting on her own eggs. He returned for the third egg and soon delivered that unborn gosling to his mate.

The fourth egg was partially hidden by sticks of the beaver lodge and the raven never discovered it. When Chelonia was cruising the shoreline that night she detected the odor of the egg. Several years before, she had found the eggs of a red-winged blackbird that had fallen into the water, and with little hesitation had made a quick meal of them. The goose egg was much larger and the shell was much thicker than that of the red-winged blackbird egg. The turtle nosed and sniffed the egg for several minutes before snapping at it with her jaws. The sharp hook on the upper jaw acted much like the beak of the raven and a small hole appeared. Chelonia snapped at the egg two more times and the yellow yolk oozed out into the water. Although the egg had little odor, the yolk triggered her hunger and she soon broke open the shell. She could not get much of the yolk in her mouth, but the embryonic gosling was pulled out and eaten in one swallow. Thus, Chelonia experienced her first meal of goose; but not her last.

The male Canada goose remained along Sand Run for the next month, but the memories of his mate faded and in early June he flew to the southern end of the Valley where he joined three other unmated geese on a large beaver pond in Mill Run.

One night in late May, a male turtle slowly swam up Sand Run toward the abandoned beaver pond where Chelonia spent most of her time. Two nights later the two turtles mated in the shallow water of the pond. Rather than retracing the path to his normal home range, the male proceeded up Sand Run. A twenty-year old female turtle had been living for the past two years in the new beaver pond, and her scent had attracted the male. The male mated with the second female, but instead of leaving he remained in the new beaver pond. The beaver had enlarged the pond to nearly two acres, large enough to support two adult turtles. Frogs, snakes, crayfish, and minnows, and several beds of pondweeds were present; there was no shortage of food for the two turtles.

The faint odor of another turtle had drifted downstream with the flowing waters of Sand Run to Chelonia on several nights. But she felt no urge to leave her home. Although prey were not always abundant there was enough to satisfy the needs of one medium-sized turtle. Sand Run supported a population of nine adult turtles, plus over thirty young ones.

Nearly four weeks after mating, Chelonia felt the urge to leave Sand Run. That one night was potentially the most dangerous of all the 365 nights of the year. When in water, Chelonia had no enemies. But when she crawled up the bank and slowly moved through the grass in search of a nesting site, she was dangerously exposed. Although small predators such as foxes and bobcats and raccoons were no threat, larger predators such as black bear and mountain lions could cause serious damage. Few predators would risk injury while attempting to make a meal of an adult snapping turtles. But as Chelonia's mother, Chelydra, had learned, the inexperienced, younger predators needed to be avoided.

Chelonia located the barren elevated knoll that she judged to be a good spot for laying eggs, and began digging the hole where she would later deposit thirty-four shiny, white eggs. After carefully covering the eggs the turtle turned toward Sand Run. Faint light had appeared over Cabin Mountain as Chelonia slowly crawled through the grass back to Sand Run. If she had been capable of hurrying she would have done so. In the dim light of dawn, she saw an animal moving close by in the grass. The animal came closer and Chelonia saw that it was blackish-brown and about the size of a large fox. It had a long, bushy tail and a somewhat pointed nose. It approached Chelonia, but instinctively avoided her jaws. She remained motionless, as was typical when any animal approached her on land.

The animal was a fisher, a member of the weasel family weighing about twelve pounds. Fisher, or black foxes as the early settlers called them, had been common throughout Canaan Valley and most of the West Virginia mountains during the 1800s. The combination of logging, fires, trapping, and clearing land, however, had wiped out all fisher in the State. In 1969 the WVDNR obtained fisher from Maine and New Hampshire and released several into Canaan Valley. Regrowth of forests and natural succession had created habitat capable of supporting a population of fisher. The goal of the reintroduction of a former resident species was to recreate the faunal community existing prior to human intervention.

Fisher are carnivores, typically feeding on red squirrels, rabbits, ruffed grouse, and wild turkey. In addition they catch mice and chipmunks, and an occasional newborn deer fawn. The health of the Canaan Valley ecosystem would never be renewed until the predator numbers were in balance with the prey numbers. It was essential that fisher and foxes, bobcats and mountain lions, and black bear and wolves return to the Valley in numbers that could control prey species, especially white-tailed deer. Because of public opinion, the WVDNR would never reintroduce timber wolves into Canaan Valley. But another wild canine would appear in the 1980s; one that would play a small role in reducing deer numbers.

Chelonia was much too large for the fisher to attack, and it continued up Sand Run in search of prey that could be easily captured with little risk of injury. The fisher would have welcomed a meal of turtle eggs, but it did not detect Chelonia's clutch that night.

CHAPTER FOURTEEN

1976-1979: BEAVER PONDS

The summer of 1976 was warmer and drier than usual and by early July water levels in the remnant of a beaver pond had decreased drastically. Water was present only in the original channel of Sand Run. There were still a few pools of water scattered nearby, but not enough to satisfy the needs of Chelonia. Prey species were scarce and with the lowering of water levels even the aquatic plants were becoming scarce. Waters trickling down Sand Run brought with them a rich variety of fascinating odors; beaver, fish, frogs, aquatic vegetation, and other snapping turtles. Chelonia was not a social animal. She did not need or want the companionship offered by other individuals. Like other snapping turtles, she gained no benefits from associating with other members of her species. Just the opposite, the more snapping turtles in a pond, the less food for each individual. But snapping turtles were not territorial; they did not defend a territory against other individuals.

Chelonia's fidelity to the abandoned beaver pond was not strong enough to outweigh the attraction of the many odors floating down Sand Run. One evening as dusk settled over the Valley, Chelonia departed the abandoned beaver pond and headed upstream. The short trip required only four hours of travel time, allowing her to pursue and capture four crayfish and a young water snake. She crawled steadily through the riffles and swam slowly through the deeper pools. She was in no hurry and although she had no actual destination she moved purposefully upstream.

As Chelonia reached the base of the beaver dam her journey was temporarily halted. If forced, she could have climbed up over the dam. But there was no reason to do so at that time. She knew that it was a simple matter to crawl around the end of the dam and thus reach the pond that the beaver had created. This pond was much larger than the pond where Chelonia had lived previously, but was nearly identical. Actually, all beaver dams and ponds in Canaan Valley were similar, with size and shape determined by the terrain. Chelonia swam slowly around the edge of the pond, foraging for food items and exploring the pond that was to be her new home. She encountered four beaver, a muskrat, and a mink before detecting the scent of another snapping turtle. The two approached cautiously and after a brief period of mutual inspection, they separated. It was another female, only twelve years old and noticeably smaller than Chelonia. Before the night was over she had made three trips around the perimeter of the pond. In so doing, she learned that there was also an adult male snapping turtle in the pond and three smaller individuals. As dawn approached she selected a depression along the side of the beaver lodge and settled in for the day.

The beaver had chosen an excellent site for their second dam on Sand Run. Water flow was adequate to keep the pond filled, but not so great as to pose a serious threat during spring runoff. And of greatest importance, there were at least five acres of aspen scattered on the bank above Sand Run. It was a relatively easy chore for them to haul the short sections of tree trunks and tree limbs downhill to the pond. Several haul trails were quite obvious, leading from aspen stand to the pond. Varying from one to two feet in width, the vegetation had been worn down to bare ground as beaver made hundreds of trips up and down the haul trails.

July, August, and then September passed quietly, and while no significant events were taking place in the beaver pond, major decisions were being made elsewhere. The Federal Power Commission had granted a license for Allegheny Power to begin construction of the Davis Power Project. When completed, the lake would flood much of the lower end of Sand Run, including the beaver pond where Chelonia resided. The beaver family, muskrats, and mink would be forced to abandon the pond. The snapping turtles, green frogs, creek chubs, and hog suckers could move upstream. The alder, viburnum, and stands of aquatic vegetation would be destroyed from inundation. Other plants and animals of Canaan Valley were in more imminent danger since at least six thousand acres of wetlands would be inundated when the lake was completely filled. The Canaan Valley ecosystem would be unalterably changed and the wetland communities would be destroyed. But several years would be required for the dam to be completed and the lake to fill. Chelonia and the other inhabitants of the beaver pond were safe for the present.

Chelonia knew nothing of the license to build the Davis Power Project and busied herself in the beaver pond, learning of the inhabitants and the best places to obtain an easy meal. She had several favorite sites along the bank where she would lie quietly, with only her nostrils and eyes above the water. With eyes strategically positioned on the top of her head, she could comfortably watch for movements along the water's edge.

To be successful in capturing prey, predators must be camouflaged, and Chelonia was no exception. Her rough, somewhat rounded upper shell resembled the many rocks that lined the banks and bottom of Sand Run. Accumulated mud and patchy moss-like growth scattered over her shell surface enabled the predatory reptile to blend in even better with her surroundings. Chelonia would often lie motionless for hours at a time, rewarded by a careless creek chub, crayfish, or water snake swimming within reach. When prey ventured within striking range, usually about five inches from her snout, Chelonia would gradually open her jaws, avoiding alarm to the unsuspecting prey. Suddenly, with mouth wide open, she would strike! The rapid head strike allowed the throat cavity to expand rapidly and created a suction that drew smaller prey into her throat. They were typically swallowed intact. She grasped larger prey items in her jaws and then slowly tore them to pieces with her strong fore-claws.

As water temperatures began to fall and frost became more common, Chelonia felt the same urge to leave the pond that had prodded her every previous autumn. Although there was a small stream flowing into the beaver pond, Chelonia did not even explore it for suitable hibernacula sites. Instead, one night in early October she crawled around the beaver dam, headed downstream, and before the eastern sky began to brighten she had moved up the small stream where she had successfully hibernated during past winters.

Chelonia emerged from her hibernaculum in April and after making her way up Sand Run she returned to the familiar beaver pond. The other two adult turtles were present, and on most days all three were in close proximity in the warm shallow water. They were drawn to the warm, quiet waters of a small cove along one side of the pond where their body temperatures slowly increased into the fifties. Days were spent basking on the sandy bank or in the shallow waters where the sun's rays heated the water, the dark mud, and the turtles. Snapping turtles do not typically bask on logs or on the stream bank, as do other aquatic turtles. Only during spring, when they are trying to raise their body temperatures do they spend any length of time resting in the sunshine. Because the lower shell covers a much smaller portion of the underside than does that of most other turtles, snapping turtles are at a greater risk of dehydration. Thus, during only a few warm days in April would Chelonia rest on the beaver lodge or on the bank of the pond.

Although air temperatures were slowly increasing as days grew longer, a late season snowstorm changed spring activities in a hurry. As ice formed on the pond, Chelonia and the other two adult turtles retreated into the mud and their activities nearly halted. The female goose that was nesting at the edge of the pond faithfully protected and warmed her five eggs, while nearly two inches of snow covered her back. The spring peepers and American toads grew quiet, and they too retreated into a state of semi-hibernation, postponing their inclinations to mate and lay eggs. A little ice and snow did not disrupt the beaver family, since their food cache contained enough branches to supply their daily meals of bark for several more weeks. Songs of male red-winged blackbirds were somewhat subdued, but they still attempted to announce and defend their territories in preparation for the return of females from their southern wintering grounds.

Slowly the monochromatic, gray-brown hillsides began to reveal promise of spring. Pink blushes of red mingled with faint blends of green throughout the hardwood hillsides, as the leaf buds of aspen, beech, black cherry, and maple began to unfurl. By the end of April another hue was added to the Valley panorama, as the deep greens of conifers were softened by thousands of white patches. The serviceberry spectacular was at a peak. The showy white flowers, which would later produce a bountiful crop of deep purple berries, created a scene that would be rivaled only by the spectacular reds and golds of the autumnal foliage. But Chelonia was not impressed. The dark murky bottom of a shallow cove, with its comfortable warm waters, was much more satisfying.

By May, water temperatures rose, and Chelonia's body temperature slowly approached sixty degrees. The second week of May was sunny and warm and she felt hungry. She had not eaten in over six months and she would feed every day during May, so long as her body temperature remained above sixty degrees. The beaver pond contained no new food items for Chelonia, but there was a plentiful supply of crayfish, green frogs, and creek chubs.

She encountered the male turtle the last week in May, during an evening feeding foray in the shallow end of the beaver pond. The two turtles had tolerated one another as they fed or basked in the shallow waters, but this meeting was different. Both turtles felt that same ancestral urge experienced by their species for millions of years. They remained near one another that night, and two nights later the male approached and aggressively began courting the female. After several attempts, during which Chelonia always moved off, he succeeded in climbing onto her back and grasping the rim of her shell with his claws. They successfully mated and forty-three eggs were fertilized.

Chelonia left the beaver pond during the second week of June and after searching along the hillside she finally located a sandy site that suited her needs. She slowly and methodically dug the flask-shaped hole that would serve during the coming months as an incubation chamber for the forty-three, tough spherical eggs. After carefully covering the eggs with sandy soil she returned to the beaver pond. Her only trip onto land had been uneventful, and she had dutifully ensured that her genes would be passed on to future turtles.

Although she had done all that was possible, it was not enough. The very next night, after the eggs were deposited, a hungry raccoon detected the scent of newly disturbed soil and he dug into the loose sand. He ate only twelve eggs that night, but returned to eat eleven more the next night. A striped skunk and a red fox each found the nest during their nightly travels and the last of the forty-three eggs was eaten by the third night. Not all turtle nests along Sand Run were destroyed by predators that summer, and the few that survived would be enough to replace the turtles that died. To maintain a stable population of snapping turtles along Sand Run, it was necessary that every adult female produce two baby turtles that would survive to maturity; one to replace the adult female and one to replace an adult male. Potential nest predators were common throughout the Sand Run drainage, and although most of Chelonia's nests had been destroyed, over two dozen of her young from previous nests had survived through their first two years. They would not reach sexual maturity until nearly twenty years old, but there would certainly be more than two of her offspring mate and lay eggs. If more than two reached mating age, the population of snapping turtles along Sand Run would slowly increase. But, if fewer than two reached mating age, the population would slowly decrease.

While she had not gone hungry in previous years, the abandoned beaver pond had not provided sufficient food for Chelonia to gain weight. For the first time in several years, Chelonia had a surplus of food. As a result, that summer her total length increased by nearly one-half inch and her weight increased over one pound. She was almost sixteen inches long and weighed nearly thirty-two pounds.

The water flowing into the beaver pond was typically clear and cool, due to the many springs and seeps that flowed out of Cabin Mountain and the middle ridge into Sand Run. It was a marked change then, when one day in early August, the waters contained noticeable amounts of silt and mud. Although the silt did not hinder Chelonia, it was a serious threat to the invertebrates that relied on clean water. For several days during August the silt was so thick in the beaver pond that Chelonia had difficulty spotting minnows and crayfish. There were enough aquatic plants growing in the beaver pond that she did not go hungry, but the mud and silt prompted her to hunt green frogs along the bank. Late one evening as she lay motionless along the shoreline, a long-legged wading bird slowly approached her from behind. The bird, a great-blue heron, was searching for food. Like the turtle, it was having difficulty spotting minnows and crayfish in the muddy water. The heron moved so slowly and cautiously that Chelonia was not aware of its presence.

Chelonia was much too large for the heron to attack; the heron actually feared adult snapping turtles. But the mud and silt had created a situation that was not typical. The heron's long black pointed bill was kept poised ready to strike at any prey spotted in the water or along the edge. The heron was one of the few animals in the Valley that could strike as rapidly as could a snapping turtle. The heron would grab small prey, such as two-inch minnows or small frogs or crayfish, but would spear larger prey. Chelonia did not see the heron as she raised her nostrils and eyes slowly out of the water. The heron could not see the turtle's head or her shell and instinctively it struck at what it thought was a small frog. The sharp bill hit just behind Chelonia's right eye and penetrated until it met solid bone. Chelonia burst through the water and the great blue heron sprung into the air, then flapped wildly from the pond. Blood flowed from Chelonia's eye as she sought the protection of the deep water next to the beaver lodge. She did not feed for nearly a week, but remained submerged much of the time. Turtles heal quickly and no infection occurred, but she lost all sight in her right eye.

The silting continued throughout September and into October, at which time Chelonia left the beaver pond and entered hibernation. Although she had no pain in the now-useless eye, she had not yet adjusted to limited sight. When striking at small prey, such as snails and crayfish, she at first missed her target. But slowly she learned to compensate for the blind eye and was as successful as ever in catching food.

The silt that led to Chelonia's injury came from construction about one-half mile up Sand Run. Chelonia had been aware of the sound of a bulldozer, but after a few days had become accustomed to the sounds of the engine and the clanking of its steel tracks. The bulldozer was building a dam across Sand Run. A private developer had purchased over one thousand acres extending from the top of Cabin Mountain to the Blackwater River and included not only the upper end of Sand Run but most of Yoakum Run. Plans called for building vacation homes and a ski resort. The Canaan Valley State Park Ski Resort had been quite successful and there was significant demand for additional recreational facilities. The natural beauty of Canaan Valley and its proximity to the heavily populated areas of Washington D.C. and northern Virginia made it a natural vacation destination.

Silt continued to flow down Sand Run throughout the winter

months, but it had almost stopped by the following summer. By 1979, the dam was completed and Sand Run Lake began to fill with water. Most of the silt had settled when it reached the beaver pond, and as a result the numbers of crayfish and snails declined. The silt did provide a good growing bed for vegetation and stands of aquatic plants soon covered shallow water around the beaver pond. While Chelonia was somewhat handicapped by the loss of sight in one eye, her sense of smell enabled her to find more than adequate amounts of plant and animal food. Life in the beaver pond returned to normal, and the beaver continued to maintain the dam and produce beaver kits each spring. Chelonia mated and deposited her clutch of eggs each year; and each year they were destroyed by predators.

CHAPTER FIFTEEN

1980-1985: WOODCOCK HUNTING AND OFF-ROAD VEHICLES

It was October 1980; the cool clear days of autumn had replaced the warm humid days of summer. Chelonia had not yet entered her hibernaculum, but it was only a matter of days before she would make her annual journey out of Sand Run and up the small stream to the submerged log that would provide shelter for the next six months. The turtle was lying within a depression beneath the undercut bank, but as always was sensitive to any unusual water movements in the pool that might signal the presence of a predator. Small waves swept into her daytime retreat, and she felt the presence of another animal in her pool. She made no effort to see the intruder, and retreated deeper into the depression.

Although the animal was larger than a bobcat, the turtle had nothing to fear. It was a bird dog, a female Brittany spaniel, with a small bell attached to the collar around her neck. The dog had been hunting hard that October morning and upon spotting Sand Run had immediately waded into the water and plopped down on her belly. She had been running through the alder and aspen thickets for nearly two hours and the cool water was a welcome relief. Because her undersides had less hair than did any other part of her body, she knew that the quickest way to cool off was to submerge the exposed belly. The orange and white dog lapped thirstily at the water while resting and cooling.

After a short time the energetic dog left the water, shook her coat, and resumed her running through the nearby alder thicket. The bell rang continuously as the dog moved along the small trickle of a stream. Suddenly the bell stopped ringing. This was a pointing dog and the strong scent of a nearby bird had brought her zig-zag sprints to a sudden halt. She lifted a front leg, stretched her neck forward toward the strong scent, and stiffened into a statue-like pose. She held the stance for nearly four minutes. During that time she remained so rigid that not even a light tinkle was produced by her bell. Suddenly a shot rang out, not the harsh blast of a twelve-gauge shotgun, but the more respectable bang of a smaller twenty-gauge. The bell immediately began ringing again, followed by a shout, "Good shot." Then another shout, "Dead bird, Bonnie, dead bird." After a few minutes of frantic searching, the Brittany spaniel located the bird, nosed it a few times, then gently picked it up and proudly brought it to her master. The young dog relinquished the bird to the senior hunter. He accepted it with genuine admiration, and after carefully examining the bill and smoothing the wing feathers he handed it to the younger hunter, his teenage son. The small brown bird was a woodcock, and was the third one the young hunter had been lucky enough to hit that morning.

After unloading their twenty-gauge, over/under shotguns, the man and his son plopped down into a bed of lycopodium, also known as ground pine, and each pulled a bag from his hunting vest. As they removed their peanut butter sandwiches the Brittany sat calmly at their feet, but her eyes were asking, if not actually begging, for a bite. As usual, both hunters gave half their sandwich to the dog, which had actually done most of the hard work that morning. With the sandwiches gone, both hunters pulled a shiny red apple from their vest and shared that with their canine, hunting companion who was so essential to the success of the trip. From previous hunts into the Valley, they knew where the best apple trees were located and they had each picked enough to satisfy themselves and the dog. Those fifty-year old trees were remnants from the farms that were once such a prominent feature of the Glade Run area. Most years, the trees produced a bountiful crop for deer and bears and hunters.

The first frost of late September had turned the bracken ferns from summer green to autumn brown. The yellow plumes of goldenrod had faded as the gaudy colors of maples dominated the hillsides. Although not deeply philosophical, the senior hunter commented that the bright fall foliage was sending a message. Just as dying campfire embers had warmed them on many occasions, the embers of summer—the gold and red and scarlet leaves—also warmed them. It was not a physical warmth, but a spiritual warming. Campfire embers sent radiant heat to their backsides, but the dazzling leaves inflamed their psyches. However, just as waning embers do not last long, the myriad hillside colors would be only a faint memory one short month later when the trees released their leaves and surrendered to earth the short-lived brilliance of October.

The man and his son had camped with their dog the night before, along Glade Run at the site of the planned power plant. The mother of the family said they were "bonding". And she was always happy for them to have the opportunity, because she understood the importance of a man and his offspring sharing those experiences.

Dew lay heavy on the grass when they left the truck early that morning, with fog swirling and undulating like a living thing across the surface of a large, nearby beaver pond. Both hunters wore blaze-orange vests and caps to confirm constantly the precise location of each to the other, even in dense fog. Ghostly geese appeared suddenly and briefly, then quickly vanished as the fog swallowed them like low-hanging clouds often swallowed the trees and boulders on Cabin Mountain. Within a few hours the sun's rays had burned off the fog, and it was obvious that the day would be warmer and drier than their canine companion preferred. Bird scent hung on the surface of the cool soil and the damp leaves; and could be readily detected by the sensitive nose of the Brittany. But the bright sunshine meant scenting conditions would quickly deteriorate and the dog would bypass many birds she would have otherwise scented.

The two hunters were enjoying one of their two or three annual hunting trips into Canaan Valley and they were not the only hunters to bring their bird dogs in pursuit of that fascinating game bird. Of all the sites east of the Mississippi where woodcock concentrated, Canaan Valley was the best known and most heavily-hunted.

During the first half of the woodcock season, usually the last two weeks of October, the only woodcock present were the residents, those birds that had returned to the Valley in March after wintering along the gulf coast. The resident population present in October consisted of the adult males and females plus the young-of-the-year that had been produced during summer. During the last half of the season, usually the first two weeks of November, the majority of the birds present were the flight birds. Those birds had spent the summer in Michigan or Maine or Canada, where they had fattened on earthworms before beginning their long autumnal migration that would end in the Gulf coastal states. Their southern voyage was triggered by the first big snowstorm of the year, when frozen ground prevented them from probing into the soil for the essential worms. Flight birds from the north and resident birds from Canaan Valley might end up sharing the same bottomland hardwoods in Louisiana or Mississippi during December and January before starting the return trip back to their northern breeding grounds.

Chelonia never saw any of the flight birds, even during their annual migration when they spent a few days or weeks in the Valley. They arrived in Canaan Valley after she had entered hibernation; on their way back they departed the Valley before she had left hibernation in the spring.

The flight birds from the north usually arrived in Canaan Valley with a cold front during the first week of November. At that time, pickup trucks with Ohio, Maryland, and Pennsylvania, and of course West Virginia, license plates were prominent in the parking lots at the Best Western Motel in Davis and the Mountain View Motel in Canaan Valley. A portable kennel was in the back of most trucks, along with hunting coats and L.L. Bean rubber-bottomed hunting boots. A few hunters chose Brittany spaniels, the most personable of all pointing dogs. Those orange-and-white or liver-and-white dogs with short tails truly enjoyed people, almost as much as they enjoyed bird hunting. Most hunters brought English setters, those long-haired, long-legged, long-tailed dogs that were big enough to crash through even the thickest spiraea patch in search of a downed woodcock or ruffed grouse. Although not quite so personable, setters did have the stamina to hunt all day, exhibiting little sign of tiring. Other pointing breeds, such as German shorthairs, accompanied some hunters during the annual pilgrimage to Canaan Valley.

Regardless of the type of hunting dog or the experience of the hunter, Canaan Valley was one of the best places in North America to hunt woodcock. In addition to woodcock, ruffed grouse and even snipe were frequently flushed while hunting. Not the least significant of the benefits of hunting in Canaan Valley was the absence of porcupines to fill a dog's mouth and face with hundreds of painful quills, and the lack of poisonous snakes to sink their deadly fangs into a careless dog. In addition, there were no ticks to attach to dogs or humans.

Woodcock hunters were not the only hunters to be attracted to Canaan Valley. Many of the same features, primarily wildlife abundance and ease of access, brought deer hunters from all parts of West Virginia and parts of Maryland, Ohio, and Pennsylvania. Bow hunters were in the Valley at the same time that woodcock hunters were present, but they usually hunted in different habitats. Turkey hunters were also present during woodcock season, but were not nearly so successful as were deer hunters or woodcock hunters. During the fall season, when both hens and gobblers could be shot, fewer than twenty birds were harvested. In contrast, fewer than ten birds were shot during the spring gobbler hunt.

Beaver attracted trappers to the many beaver ponds scattered around the Valley. Those trappers, mostly local individuals, removed a few beaver, muskrat, and mink each year. Even though a trapper set his traps near the beaver dams along Sand Run, Chelonia had nothing to fear. She was isolated in her hibernaculum, which was located nearly two hundred yards from the closest beaver dam. But even if she had chosen a hibernaculum within the beaver dam, her total lack of activity would have prevented her from coming close to a beaver trap. Hunters and trappers had minimal impact on Chelonia and other snapping turtles, but other outdoor enthusiasts were a different matter.

After emerging from her hibernaculum in 1985, Chelonia mated with the male turtle that inhabited the same stretch of Sand Run. Her annual June trek from the stream to the nearby hillside, where she deposited forty-five round white eggs, was stressful but uneventful. However, when only a few yards from Sand Run on her return trip, she heard a disturbing noise approaching from the direction of Glade Run. Chelonia had heard the noise several times in the past, but it had never approached close enough for her to actually see what caused it. This day would be different.

While on the bank above Sand Run she saw an object unlike anything she had ever witnessed. It was roaring along Sand Run, smashing through the spiraea and goldenrod and alder. It splashed through a small stream that entered Sand Run, then crossed Sand Run where the water was less than one foot deep. Chelonia moved as quickly as possible to the stream edge and plopped into the water. This was not a black bear, or mountain lion, or any other wild animal; it was an all-terrain vehicle. The ATV, as it was commonly called, was a four-wheeler carrying two humans. It was followed by five other ATVs. The riders were covered with mud from head to toe, a by-product of the many bogs and streams and mud holes they had crashed through that morning.

Luckily for Chelonia and other snapping turtles of Sand Run, the ATV riders were not looking for turtles. They were engaged in the sport of recreational riding, made more challenging, enjoyable, and muddier by the numerous wetlands and bogs scattered across the Valley floor. The only direct threat to snapping turtles was when they were encountered on land in the process of egg laying.

The riders were following segments of the abandoned railroad grade that crossed Sand Run at two locations and paralleled it for much of its length. After the ATVs had disappeared up Sand Run and the disturbing roar of their four-stroke engines had faded away, Chelonia cautiously swam down Sand Run to the safety of the beaver pond where she felt secure against any intruders. Chelonia searched for food as she moved toward the beaver pond, but the water was so muddied by the ATVs that she could not see the minnows or crayfish that were present in that stretch of stream. The mud and silt reached the beaver pond a few hours later and the pond waters remained so muddy, that for three days Chelonia was unable to capture a meal. June was the month when snapping turtles consumed the greatest amount of food and the month when they replenished all those body reserves lost during hibernation. It was also the month they began to accumulate reserves for the coming winter.

Other animals were also impacted by the ATVs, some more seriously than others. Hundreds of tadpoles and salamander larvae had been directly killed by the six ATVs, while thousands of other aquatic animals would suffer from the life-threatening silt. Eggs of snails and crayfish and various other invertebrates would be covered with silt, and the oxygen they were so dependent on would be greatly reduced. Even those animals dwelling on the banks above Sand Run did not escape unharmed. One ATV crushed the eggs of a late-nesting female mallard, while another spilled the eggs from the nest of a swamp sparrow. Raccoons and skunks would find easy meals that night.

Off-road vehicle use had been increasing steadily since 1975, when the Blackwater 100, an annual motorcycle race, was held in Canaan Valley. An ATV race had been added to the annual event in 1983, and the riders along Sand Run that June day in 1985 were practicing for the upcoming race. The twenty-mile course crossed rivers and bogs, beaver ponds and mud holes. The first Blackwater 100 attracted 395 entrants, and by 1985, five hundred racers entered the motorcycle race while an additional three hundred participated in the ATV race. The two-day event, billed as "America's Toughest Race", attracted thirty thousand spectators. The actual layout of the racecourse changed each year, and in so doing, spread even broader impacts over all sections of the northern end of Canaan Valley.

While the Blackwater 100 was restricted to two days in June, off-road vehicles were present from April through November. Only when deep snows and bitter cold descended upon the Valley, were they absent. For the riders, the grades of the long-abandoned railroads were the greatest attraction. The solid bases of rocks and cinders, and even wooden ties in some sections, provided prominent trails from Davis to Glade Run, through the Little Blackwater and the North Branch. Motorcycles, three-wheelers, four-wheelers, jeeps, and raised pickup trucks with oversized tires traversed every mile of the grades that had once been common courses for Shay engines.

If off-road vehicles had been restricted to the railroad grades, their impacts would have been minimal. But most ATVs did not remain on the grades, especially during the Blackwater 100 race. Although no scientific studies had been conducted to document the impacts of off-road vehicles, by 1985 the U.S. Fish and Wildlife Service and WVDNR had concluded that the adverse impacts sustained by the natural resources of Canaan Valley were quite significant.

A key attraction of Canaan Valley for hunters and trappers and ATV enthusiasts was the availability of unposted land and the intriguing landscape. Monongahela Power Company had never posted its property since it was purchased in the early 1920s; hunters and off-road vehicles could therefore wander unchecked throughout the Power Company's lands as well as those of Western Pocahontas Properties—wherever and whenever they wanted. The entire northern two-thirds of the Valley, nearly twenty thousand acres, contained no houses and was open to hunting and ATV riding. The dirt road from State Route 93 to the site of the proposed power plant along Glade Run provided access to all of the lands between the Blackwater River and Cabin Mountain, including areas along Sand Run, Glade Run, and the Little Blackwater River. Access into the northern end of the Valley was possible from several points: along the Blackwater River from Davis; off the mountain at Canaan Heights; from Cortland Road into the North Branch watershed; and into the Sand Run area from a dirt road that passed the Beall farm.

Late October in Canaan Valley was arguably the best time of the year for bird hunters, hikers, and other outdoor enthusiasts. The nights were chilly or downright cold, but the days usually warmed to shirtsleeve temperatures. Mosquitoes and deer flies were no longer pests, blueberries were ripe, and hundreds of springs flowing from the hillsides provided cool drinks to humans and their canine companions. The aspens, both bigtooth and quaking, transformed to golden yellow, shimmered and trembled with even the slightest breeze.

It was nearly impossible to get lost in Canaan Valley; unless the fog settled in for the day, or a snowstorm swept in and obliterated the mountains. The openness of the Valley floor provided vistas that were highly unusual for most of the central Appalachians, with unlimited visibility of more than two miles. Most streams flowed north before turning west toward Davis, and the mountains that surrounded the Valley floor provided prominent landmarks that even the most inexperienced hikers and hunters could use to guide them back to their starting points. But in spite of these landmarks, some hunters and hikers—even those who carried a compass—had gotten lost and not been able to find their vehicle until many hours after darkness settled in, or even the next day. But unlike Dolly Sods where the weather could become life threatening, the possibility of a Canaan Valley outing ending in someone's death was highly unlikely.

Another feature of the Valley that benefited wildlife as well as hunters was the diversity of habitats. Fifty years of plant succession had resulted in an interspersion of habitat types unlike any other in the central Appalachians. Rather than expansive stands of hardwoods, which covered much of the region around Canaan, the Valley was characterized by thousands of distinct patches, many smaller than one hundred acres. The stands of aspen and alder were most important to woodcock because of the large earthworm populations they supported. But the mosaic of plant communities, dominated by spiraea, hardwoods, conifers, muskeg, grassland, and beaver pond complexes, was also important. The great diversity of wildlife that populated Canaan Valley was attributable to the great diversity of habitat types distributed throughout the Valley.

Disturbance usually results in increased biodiversity. This is true for natural disturbances such as floods, blow-downs, or fires, and it was true for the human-caused disturbance that had been thrust upon Canaan Valley. The plant communities that follow disturbances are radically different from the plant communities that existed prior to the disturbances. Biodiversity in Canaan Valley would become greater in the coming decades than it had ever been prior to the logging and fires.

Chelonia and the other snapping turtles that inhabited the various bodies of water on the floor of Canaan Valley were not directly influenced by the diversity of habitats. Other than the river, its major tributaries, and the larger beaver ponds, the other habitats played a minor role in their natural history. Females did need suitable sites for egg laying and all turtles needed suitable sites for hibernating. Certainly the other habitats indirectly affected the lives of all snapping turtles, especially the younger ones.

A key factor in the survival of snapping turtles was the abundance of great blue herons, ravens, raccoons, fisher, mink, foxes, bobcats, and black bears. The abundance and diversity of prey species, both upland and wetland, led to an abundance and diversity of predators. The lives of Chelydra and Chelonia had been closely intertwined with the lives of all other animal species that existed in this mountain valley. A stable ecosystem, such as that existing in Canaan Valley, must have a balance of both prey species and predator species to function and perpetuate.

Natural plant succession following the ruinous logging of the early 1900s had produced a steady improvement of wildlife habitat, but the development of certain types of habitat was determined by human activity. While ecological succession progressed at a steady and somewhat predictable rate, the influence of humans was erratic and unpredictable. The replacement of conifer communities by aspen stands, and the repeated renewal of those stands by beaver had created near-optimum woodcock habitat. From 1930 to 1970, large numbers of cattle and sheep ranged freely throughout much of the northern end of Canaan. These animals aided in the creation of prime woodcock habitat by controlling the growth of dense woody vegetation and by depositing thousands of manure piles throughout the aspen and alder thickets. The earthworms attracted to the manure piles were a prime food source, and the grazing maintained a low ground cover, which was much preferred by woodcock.

Woodcock numbers peaked by 1980, and by 1985 they were lower than during the 1970s, due primarily to the loss of suitable habitat. A key factor leading to the decline of habitat was the removal of livestock from much of the Valley. Woodcock numbers in Canaan Valley would never again be as high as were those of the 1960s and 1970s.

CHAPTER SIXTEEN

1986-1990: SAND RUN LAKE

The beaver family had trouble finding adequate aspen to bolster their food cache during the fall of 1986 and were forced to travel more than two hundred yards from Sand Run to reach aspen trees. After cutting them into short lengths that could be dragged back to the pond they faced a somewhat perilous trip, not once but dozens of times each night. In Canaan Valley few predators existed that could kill a beaver, but nighttime was the period of greatest risk. Timber wolves had once been a common predator of beaver in Canaan Valley, but that was nearly two hundred years earlier. A few beaver were killed each year by black bears, but the sharp incisors that could cut down a large tree could also inflict serious injury to the foot of a black bear.

One night in early November as the beaver were working long hours to complete their food cache, a large predator capable of easily killing an adult beaver moved quietly up Sand Run. The adult male beaver was skillfully removing the last large chips from the base of an aspen. The adult female had just hauled a large aspen branch into the pond and was busy inserting it into the food cache. The yearlings, nearly seventeen months old, were busy repairing the dam and moving small aspen branches that the adults brought to the pond. The young-of-the-year, nearly five months old, remained in the pond; playing, chewing bark from the tender branches, and hauling small branches around the pond.

The predator detected beaver scent as it approached the dam and heard the aspen tree fall as the male beaver cut through the base. It had successfully hunted beaver several times and associated the chewing and the falling aspen with those large rodents. The predator was a mountain lion, also known as cougar or puma. The large 160-pound male did most of his hunting on Dolly Sods, and his home range covered more than one hundred square miles. The explosion of deer numbers had provided an abundance of preferred food and the large cat seldom left Dolly Sods. Once or twice a year it visited the remote sections of Canaan Valley, where deer, groundhogs, and beaver provided easy meals. Mountain lions had been common throughout Canaan Valley and most of West Virginia prior to the arrival of settlers, but the large cats were nearly wiped out by 1850.

A well-meaning individual from Baltimore, Maryland had released this particular male near Bear Rocks, at the northern end of Dolly Sods. The individual had visited Dolly Sods several times to watch hawks and pick blueberries and concluded that the remote area was an ideal place for mountain lions, if they did not already live there. After much searching, he finally located a dealer who had a young mountain lion that had been raised in captivity. As with many captive cats, once it had grown past the cute stage the owners no longer wanted the animal. The cat was nearly two years old that afternoon in May when it was released from the back of a pickup truck. It immediately headed for the great boulder field and quickly disappeared from sight.

The male wandered widely over Dolly Sods and adjoining areas, sometimes dropping down toward the South Branch River, sometimes over to the Stony River dam site. It ranged south to the Roaring Plains and west into Canaan Valley. Deer fawns provided easy meals during May and June and by late summer it had learned to hunt older deer. The male cougar typically killed one deer every week and supplemented that with an occasional beaver or groundhog, which it often killed as much for fun as for hunger. There were no other mountain lions in the Dolly Sods region during the first year following the cat's release, although the individual from Baltimore had located a young female that he hoped to release the next year. As the young male neared sexual maturity, the drive to find a female drove him to wander widely throughout his normal home range. Although he constantly marked his territory at scent posts, no other cougar had detected his sign.

The mountain lion had learned quickly to avoid humans and retreated into the most inaccessible spots on Dolly Sods when hawk-watchers or blueberry pickers or deer hunters were present. Most days were spent in the shelter of fields with car-sized boulders, a prominent feature of the western border of Dolly Sods. He spent morning hours sprawled out lazily atop one of the large flat rocks, then retreated into the cool darkness of a cave-like opening during the mid-day hours. On one or two rare occasions he was spotted as he crossed the dirt road running the length of Dolly Sods, but no deer hunter ever spotted him long enough to get a shot.

The U. S. Fish and Wildlife Service listed the eastern mountain lion as an endangered species, and it would have been a serious crime for someone to kill the big cat. Though raised in captivity, it was still protected by federal law. Ironically, the person who had released the mountain lion had broken the law in doing so. It was illegal to release any wild animal in West Virginia, even if the animal was raised in captivity.

The male beaver was upwind of the mountain lion and was occupied with removing the limbs from the aspen tree. The lion did not see the beaver, but its strong scent told the cat exactly where it was located. The cat stalked to within fifteen feet and in two bounds was on top of it. The cougar's four long sharp canines pierced the neck of the beaver before it had a chance to move. The fifty-pound beaver provided two meals for the mountain lion, which two days later returned to Dolly Sods.

The beaver family fortunately had completed the food cache and the remaining members had no problem surviving winter. The lodge and dam were in good shape and the adult female, with the assistance of the two yearlings, easily completed any repair work that was needed. With one less adult to feed, the food cache was more than enough to get them through winter. However, the distance to available aspen was a serious problem.

All remaining members of the beaver family survived winter, as did Chelonia and the two other adult turtles in the Sand Run beaver pond. Bark from the food cache lasted through May, but when all had been consumed the beaver faced a long-range problem. Succulent aquatic plants would provide adequate food through the summer months, but available aspen was too scarce and too far removed from the beaver pond. The adult female left the pond in July and was followed by the remaining four family members. Normally, the yearlings would have been forced out of the colony in May, but the adult female was not pregnant that spring and the youngsters were allowed to stay.

They soon reached the beaver pond that had been abandoned nearly ten years ago, and carefully inspected the remains of their lodge and dam. The dam was almost completely destroyed, and the lodge had caved in and was uninhabitable. However, aspen on the hillside that had been severely clearcut by the beaver during their years at that site had grown back. The root suckers had grown into trees that were over twenty feet tall and more than six inches in diameter at the base. The amazing regrowth abilities of the aspen had produced a large stand of trees that could once again support a small beaver colony.

The entire beaver family set to work, as only beaver can do, rebuilding the dam and the lodge. As yearlings, the youngsters were skilled in cutting trees, hauling branches, and carrying mud to reinforce the dam and lodge. By August, the pond had increased to nearly half an acre in size and the fall rains would make it even larger. During September, an adult male beaver wandered up Sand Run and with a minimum of courtship was soon accepted as a member of the family. Although there had been no beaver kits born to the colony that year, there would almost certainly be new additions the following spring.

As with most beaver ponds, the abandoned one where Chelonia lived slowly decreased in size. Piece by piece, the sticks and mud gave way until a steady stream of water flowed over the dam. In spite of the leaks, the pond would remain adequate that summer to support the thriving wildlife community of previous years. A family of muskrats lived in the abandoned beaver lodge, while water snakes, green frogs, American toads, creek chubs, crayfish, and snails all continued the cycle of living and dying. There is, at best, an uneasy harmony between individuals in Nature. Competition and predation leave little opportunity for harmony. But populations of predators and prey along Sand Run were in balance. Prey species produced a surplus of young, while predator species were maintained at a low enough level so that they would not wipe out the all-important prey species.

Chelonia played an important role in maintaining the balance of the beaver pond community. She produced a surplus of eggs and young that provided food for the resident predators, while she herself acted as a predator to control numbers of prey species. The diversity of habitats throughout Canaan Valley was a key element in maintaining the balance of predators and prey so critical to a balanced ecosystem.

The second summer following the abandonment of the beaver pond, water levels dropped so low that the pond was not producing enough food for the adult turtles. They frequently encountered one another while feeding, and on several occasions Chelonia had been attacked by the male when they both were after an injured creek chub. The small stream of water that flowed down Sand Run brought with it a very attractive blend of odors from Sand Run Lake. Even before the lake had completely filled with water, several thousand large-mouth bass and bluegill were introduced. The flooded vegetation provided an abundance of food for invertebrates such as snails and crayfish, which in turn provided an abundance of food for the bass and bluegill. Consistent with newly created lakes, fish populations expanded rapidly due to the availability of cover and food.

Chelonia abandoned the beaver pond one evening in August and headed upstream, drawn to the attractive mixture of odors that promised an abundance of food. She reached the base of the dam while stars still dominated the night sky, but made no attempt to climb over or around the dam. There was a deep pool of water below the outtake pipe draining the lake, and she spent the next day in a natural cavity under the bank. After darkness had fallen she began the slow journey up the fifty-yard face of the earthen dam. She moved easily through the grass that been seeded on the dam and in less than one hour she plopped into the waters of Sand Run Lake.

Although the lake was not large compared to other lakes throughout West Virginia, it covered more than thirty acres. With dimensions of one hundred yards by half a mile, the extensive shorelines were important to Chelonia. She began her exploration almost immediately. Following the western shoreline she slowly swam and crawled along the bank. Water was roughly fifteen feet deep at the dam, but graduated to less than one foot deep at the upper end. Grasses, sedges, rushes, and cattails lined the shoreline around most of the lake, and alder thickets grew at the edge of shallow waters in the upper end. The southeastern corner contained a flooded stand of red spruce and balsam fir, many of which had died and fallen into the lake. Seven small streams flowed from the adjacent hillsides into small coves that were scattered around the lake, and Sand Run flowed through a well-defined channel into the shallow upper end of the lake. A family of beaver had built a dam about two hundred yards upstream of the lake and the resulting pond added to the broad expanse of open water that was to be Chelonia's home.

To be optimum habitat for snapping turtles a lake must provide abundant food, plus adequate protective cover in the form of trees and shrubs. The dead tops of flooded alders emerged from the lake in several places and Chelonia moved slowly along the shoreline exploring every rock and log and cove she encountered. She had covered only a small section of shoreline when the first rays of sunlight spread over Cabin Mountain. Fog lay heavy over the lake and the excitement of a new home caused Chelonia to continue her exploration. She wandered into a small cove that had overgrown banks and several ideal-hiding places. Moving into the shallows, she selected a depression where she could safely spend the daylight hours.

Chelonia was hungry, and the mixture of tantalizing odors was so strong that she left the cove and began feeding as the sun slowly receded over the treeline of the middle ridge. Hundreds of small fish, mainly young bluegill, were feeding in the shallow water. In less than thirty minutes she had captured four, more than enough to satisfy her hunger. Continuing her slow cautious travel, she moved into another cove filled with the dead tops of flooded alders. While Chelonia picked her way through these alders she noticed dozens of large crayfish climbing on the stems. Unable to resist the easy meal, she quickly caught and ate six of the tasty crustaceans. She encountered bass, bluegill, and black bullhead catfish, more fish than she had seen in her life.

Food was abundant and there was no shortage of hiding places, ideal habitat for a snapping turtle. Chelonia explored most of the lake during the next two months, resting many hours in the flooded trees along the southeastern edge of the lake. When the lake was filling, a small stand of red spruce and balsam fir succumbed within a year. Many of them fell into the water, creating ideal resting cover for Chelonia.

By September, Chelonia had encountered forty-nine adult snapping turtles in the lake. There were also several dozen smaller turtles, but they spent most of their time in the thick cover unthreatened by predators. By early October, Chelonia noticed that several turtles had left the lake and although she did not know where they had gone, she was aware of unusually strong turtle odors flowing out of several small streams that flowed into the lake. As the urge to hibernate became stronger, she swam up Sand Run through the beaver pond and then moved up a stream flowing from the base of Cabin Mountain. She passed two turtles hibernating under the roots of an alder clump, then passed another under an old spruce log. About two hundred yards from the lake she came to a large submerged hemlock log. There was a shallow depression under the log and water flowed through in a steady stream. Crawling under the log she dug a few inches into the soft mud. The water was about eight inches deep and when submerged in the mud Chelonia was able to extend the end of her nose out of the water. The water was much cooler than the lake and within a few days Chelonia's body temperature had dropped to forty-five degrees. Her body processes slowed appreciably and she entered the first stage of hibernation. Water flowing past her dropped to thirty-four degrees by December and she absorbed all the oxygen she needed from the water that flowed over and around her body.

Although the stream flowing out of Cabin Mountain warmed only slightly in March, Chelonia somehow sensed that it was nearly time for her to leave her hibernaculum and return to the lake. The first week of April found Chelonia basking in the shallow waters at the upper end of Sand Run Lake. Sunlight heated the water; Chelonia and all the other turtles that had concentrated in the shallow waters began to slowly increase their activities. By the middle of April temperatures of turtles and shallow waters had reached sixty degrees and the spring feeding forays began.

Bluegill and bass fingerlings provided easy meals, while crayfish were eaten daily. But there were other foods available to Chelonia as she slowly cruised the shoreline. Early one morning she was moving through the shallow grasses in a small cove when she spotted a Canada goose swimming toward her. As the goose came closer, Chelonia stopped then slowly submerged and partially buried in the mud and muck that covered most the lake floor. Her head was four inches under the water when the mother goose passed. Close behind her came five goslings. The babies had hatched only one week earlier and were still covered with the soft, greenish-yellow down feathers that characterized baby ducks and geese. Four of the goslings swam closely behind their mother but the fifth wandered some distance away.

The goslings were searching for any insects or tadpoles small enough for them to capture. Although geese parents did not feed their young they led them to places where food was abundant. The shallow waters of the many coves scattered around Sand Run Lake were ideal brood habitat, except for covert hazards. One minute the fifth gosling was paddling slowly in front of Chelonia and the next minute it had disappeared from sight. The gosling died in the powerful jaws of the turtle, and Chelonia experienced another new food.

Chelonia caught and ate four more goslings during the next week but as the young geese grew, their diet switched from invertebrates to grasses. Adults and goslings spent daylight hours searching for succulent grasses and newly formed seed heads. As a result they spent little time in the waters of the lake. But there were other foods for the snapping turtles that cruised the shoreline of Sand Run Lake.

Newly hatched ducklings of mallards, black ducks, and wood ducks were also in the lake. Wood ducks eggs were laid in the cavities of hollow trees along the shoreline, and after hatching the ducklings jumped directly into the water. Mallards and black ducks laid their eggs in the tall grasses around the lake and then brought their young to the lake shortly after they hatched. Ducklings, like the goslings, searched for the protein-rich invertebrates essential for their early growth and survival. Ducklings were even easier to capture than were goslings. The baby ducks fed on invertebrates for over one month and did not move onto land to feed as did the goslings. Also, goslings grew so rapidly that by the time they were four weeks old they were almost too large for Chelonia to capture. In spite of the ease of capturing ducklings, they were not favored food for Chelonia or any other snapping turtles, no matter how easy to catch. Fish were their favorite.

Bass and bluegill were eaten regularly, but Chelonia typically caught only fingerlings. Adults were too wary and too large for her to catch easily. But that changed when the bluegill began spawning during the middle of May. Adult bluegill congregated at spawning beds located at six sites around Sand Run Lake, and Chelonia soon learned where each of those was located. In the shallow waters, usually six to ten inches deep, adult bluegill created depressions, or nests, where eggs were deposited. Males concentrated around these depressions, which were often situated less than twelve inches apart, and it was not unusual to have thirty or forty male bluegill defending their territories in a spawning bed.

Chelonia discovered that she could lie patiently at the outer edge of a spawning bed and be rewarded when a careless bluegill swam within striking range. Although her strike and subsequent capture disrupted spawning activities, bluegill soon forgot about the commotion and resumed normal behavior. Chelonia frequently ate two or three adult bluegill before moving away from the spawning beds to a resting place where she could digest her meal. Spawning typically lasted for only two or three weeks, and by June the easy bluegill meals had ended for the year. But finding enough food was never a problem for Chelonia. In addition to crayfish, green frogs and water snakes were quite abundant. Chelonia even managed to catch a young muskrat that had carelessly ventured out of its bank den two weeks before it was weaned from the mother.

In July, Chelonia began to notice dozens, then hundreds of feathers floating in the lake. At first she thought they might possibly be food, but she determined that even though they might smell like a goose they couldn't really be eaten. At the same time she noticed the feathers, she observed that the geese had formed one large flock of over forty birds. The thousands of feathers that floated around the lake were not from dead geese, but had been molted by the geese that were growing new sets of feathers.

Most birds lose their feathers one or two at a time and new ones grow in within a few days. As a result, they never lose the ability to fly. In contrast, geese and ducks lose all of their flight feathers at the same time. By the first week of July none of the geese on Sand Run Lake, or any other place in Canaan Valley, could fly. They could swim and run, but they could not fly. All of the long sturdy wing feathers that were capable of carrying them from Canada to Texas had been molted. Ornithologists had given this new set of feathers the name, eclipse plumage. Mallards, black ducks, and wood ducks, the only three species of ducks that nested in Canaan Valley, also acquired their eclipse plumage at the same time. None were capable of flying.

The new flight feathers grew in quickly, but it would be nearly one month before the geese were capable of flying again. By the end of July, adult geese were running and paddling and flapping awkwardly across the surface of the lake as they tried to regain their powers of flight. The goslings had molted their plumage of down feathers and by the end of July the long stiff wing feathers were strong enough to support them in flight. Goslings began to imitate the adults and their clumsy flying and landing improved steadily until they could accompany the adults on their practice flights around the lake. By August all geese were capable of flight and they frequently left the lake in search of fields of succulent grasses elsewhere in the Valley. Predictably they would return to Sand Run Lake as twilight arrived and flock after flock of geese landed noisily in the lake where they spent the night.

Chelonia was unaware that geese left the Valley during winter. They were present when she entered hibernation and present when she emerged from her hibernaculum. She never saw them leave or return. The deep snows and frozen waters forced the geese to leave the Valley each year. They remained through September and October, even though snows fell and skim ice formed on the beaver ponds. The first full moon in November typically triggered their departure. After the moon had climbed high into the sky, the various flocks of geese lifted off the water and after circling a few times formed into the V-shape so characteristic of the majestic birds. With the point of the "V" aimed toward Red Creek, the birds flew over Weiss Knob and headed southeast. Their destination was North Carolina. They arrived there before daylight and settled in around the coastal marsh that would be their home during the next three months.

Canada geese typically mate for life and one of the most important events that took place on the wintering grounds was the selection of mates. Two-year old geese formed pairs while adults solidified their pair bonds. Any birds that had lost their mates during the previous year found new ones before they left North Carolina.

Geese arrived back in Canaan Valley during the first week of March. Those that had nested the previous year moved to that same site and immediately began to defend the area against other pairs. Within three weeks the females had constructed nests and by the first week of April most were sitting on a clutch of eggs. The annual cycle of egg laying, incubation, and hatching started once again. The release of Canada geese into Canaan Valley by the WVDNR had been successful and in less than twenty years the numerous beaver ponds had attracted nesting birds to all parts of the Valley.

CHAPTER SEVENTEEN

1991-1995: TURTLES AND WILDLIFE RESEARCH

The last two hours of daylight offered nature's greatest show. Diurnal wildlife, those that were active during daylight hours, were completing their last meal of the day and beginning to move toward their nighttime retreats. Nocturnal wildlife, whose activities occurred during nighttime hours, were departing their daytime retreats and venturing out to begin their feeding forays. Because those activities overlapped during evening hours, a greater variety of wildlife was active than at any other time during the twenty-four hour cycle.

Mallards and wood ducks were seeking the shelter of dense marsh vegetation and flooded alder thickets. Canada geese completed their grazing on succulent grasses and noisily swam out into the open lake where the risk of predation was greatly reduced. Great blue herons, flying with slow but strong wing beats, headed for the tops of tall spruce trees where they perched until daylight wakened them. Crows headed for their roosts in tall hemlocks where they were partially protected from the nighttime attacks of barred owls.

Tree swallows were constantly dipping and diving over the lake's insect-rich surface to capture their last meal before darkness forced them into shelter among the alders. Cedar waxwings perched hawk-like in dead snags along the shoreline watching intently for unsuspecting insects that would become their last meal of the day.

The swallows, waxwings, and nighthawks were gradually replaced by bats, which were attracted to the night insects. Like the bats, the insects had emerged from their daytime retreats to seek nourishment. An occasional nighthawk dived with roaring wings after mosquitoes that were searching for a meal of blood from an unsuspecting mammal or bird. Muskrats and beaver left their dens to search for the tender vegetation that nourished them during summer months. Green frogs, the largest frogs in Canaan Valley, began their chorus of twanged rubber band calls that would continue throughout the night. Snapping turtles likewise began their evening activities. Although some turtle movement occurred sporadically throughout daylight hours, the period of greatest activity occurred during the hours of darkness. During that time they patrolled the shallow shoreline for frogs or water snakes, crayfish or bluegills, ducklings or baby muskrats.

That particular July evening started the same as had hundreds of other summer nights for Chelonia, but it would be unlike any other she had experienced. She left her daytime retreat that was located under the stems of a submerged alder, killed by the lake waters flooding the wetlands bordering Sand Run. A nighttime breeze blowing out of the south caused a slight rippling of the lake surface and the strong scent of fish flesh was carried along the shoreline. Chelonia had been cruising the shoreline for over thirty minutes when she detected the odor. Following the invisible scent trail, she slowly zeroed in on the irresistible odor. Several other lake residents also detected the fish odor, but Chelonia was the first to arrive. She could swim faster than most other animals in the lake and her sense of smell was more acute than any other aquatic animal. With the aid of a slight breeze, Chelonia could detect the scent of an injured fish with torn flesh at distances of forty yards.

On that particular July night she hurried toward the odor with hopes of obtaining an easy meal. She approached within six feet of the fish when she encountered another turtle. With a warning bite to its hind leg, she aggressively threatened the smaller, nine-pound male and forced it to give way as she approached. The fish, actually only the heads of five bluegill, were lying in the shallow water and were available for the taking.

During her life in Sand Run Lake she had eaten many bluegill heads that had been thrown into the lake by successful fisherman. Sensing no danger, she moved within ten inches then cautiously extended her muscular head to clamp sharp powerful jaws onto the fish. As she took one more step her front foot pressed down on something strangely smooth and solid. There was a splash behind her and she felt something strike the back of her shell. Reacting immediately, she tried to back up but her way was blocked. She attempted to turn right, then left, and then straight ahead. But at each turn she met something solid. The same solid resistance was under her feet and over her head.

Although Chelonia did not know it, she was being held prisoner in a turtle trap; the type used by commercial trappers who harvested snapping turtles for specialty restaurants. Harvesting snapping turtles was legal in West Virginia and in most states throughout the range of the snapping turtle. In some northern states over ten thousand snapping turtles were trapped each year and made into turtle soup. Was this to be the outcome that fate had in store for Chelonia?

She had never before been entrapped and continued to push against the wire sides as she would have pushed against the stems of flooded alder bushes. But this time her strength did not let her bulldoze past the obstruction. She continued to probe with her nose and dig with her claws, but to no avail. The trap was sturdy and well designed and no turtle had ever escaped after the door dropped shut. The trap was twelve inches high, twenty-four inches wide, and thirty-six inches long, allowing plenty of room for Chelonia to turn around. After twenty minutes of constant probing she seemed to accept the situation and directed her attention to the bluegill heads. She tore off pieces and ate enough to satisfy her immediate hunger. After a few more attempts to escape the trap she settled onto the bottom. Her small brain did not recognize any danger. Food was available and the top of the trap extended two inches above the water, thus she could easily extend her nose to breath. She consumed all of one bluegill head and part of another during that short summer night. She continued to make a few feeble attempts to push through the wire, but did not exert her full strength. She never used her powerful jaws to bite the trap wire; such action would have had no effect on the trap's heavy twelve-gauge wire.

Chelonia might have expressed frustration, but not fear. Turtles and other cold-blooded animals have no comprehension of death. They respond to threats from larger predators, not because they are aware that they might be injured or killed, but because instinct directs them to protect themselves. Thus they respond to the best of their physical ability.

As darkness began to fade and dawn faintly appeared over Cabin Mountain, Chelonia renewed her efforts to escape the trap. She normally would not have remained in the shallows when daylight arrived and thus a sense of urgency spurred her to greater efforts. She braced her hind legs against the bottom of the trap and pushed the front edge of her shell against the top of the trap. Although she managed to bend the top outward nearly two inches, her efforts were wasted.

As the sun came over Cabin Mountain, Chelonia sank to the bottom of the trap that was resting on the lake bottom. She retreated to the bottom not to escape the sunlight, because it would not cause her any physical harm, but because she felt vulnerable in the shallow water. After the sun had climbed thirty degrees over Cabin Mountain Chelonia sensed a movement in the water. She could sense slight changes of water pressure and movements of water over her shell as something approached. Then she saw it—a canoe. She had seen many canoes in the lake, but had always avoided them by diving to the bottom when one approached within twenty or thirty yards. Although no harm had ever resulted from an encounter with a canoe, her instincts warned her to avoid them. The resemblance to large crocodiles that preyed on ancestral snapping turtles millions of years ago might have been the basis for her natural apprehension. Or did the combined form of canoe and human trigger inherited memories of a long-extinct aquatic dinosaur?

Chelonia did not rush wildly around the trap as would a squirrel or raccoon or bird. Instead she remained motionless as she did when any large predator approached. But this predator did not pass her by, instead the human climbed out of the canoe and waded toward the trap. He eyed the large turtle with satisfaction then lifted the trap from the water. With much difficulty, he hoisted the fifty pounds of turtle and trap into the canoe.

Chelonia remained motionless on the bottom of the trap as the human paddled the canoe through the marsh grass and across the lake. Upon reaching the opposite shore he stepped out and pulled the canoe up onto the bank. With much difficulty, he lifted the trapped turtle out of the canoe and carried it to a relatively flat grassy site. After propping open the door he raised the back end of the trap and shook it until the turtle began falling toward the open door. Although she grasped the wire with her long claws he pried them loose and she slowly slid out of the trap onto the ground. If she had been in the water she could have escaped. She realized that her jaws, and not her legs, were her only means of survival. As the human moved around her she turned so that her head was constantly facing him. As he stepped closer she suddenly snapped viciously at his foot. Having trapped many turtles, the human knew the length of her neck and kept just out of reach of the powerful jaws.

The man took a tape measure from his tool box, measured the length and width and height of Chelonia's upper shell, and took care to avoid the snapping jaws. After recording those measurements, he used a canoe paddle to divert her attention. Then he stepped behind her and quickly grabbed her by the tail. Although her tail was shorter than that of most other turtles, due to an earlier attack by a large mink, it was long enough for the human to get a firm hold. He picked up the turtle and placed her headfirst into a large plastic bucket. Suspending the bucket from a set of scales attached to a tripod, he determined that the turtle weighed forty-one pounds.

He recorded the weight, carried her to a large bucket that was upside down on the ground, and maneuvered her so that she was lying upside down on top of the bucket. Her legs and head extended beyond the sides and although she struggled she could not move off the top of the bucket.

The man opened a plastic tool box, pulled out a metal file and a battery-powered drill, then drilled two small holes in the edge of the turtle's shell near a left hind leg. Next he filed two small v-shaped notches on the other side of the shell. Because the edge of a turtle's shell was a combination of bone and chitin no blood came from the notches or the drilled holes. The turtle kicked several times while the notches were being filed and the small holes were being drilled, but she remained nearly motionless after the operations were completed.

From a padded box the man removed a four-inch long transmitter with an eight-inch long antennae. He attached it to the rear edge of the turtle's shell using two brass bolts inserted through the previously drilled small holes. He measured the precloaca length and the posterior lobe of the plastron plate on the underside of the turtle and, because the precloacal length was shorter, the man recorded the turtle as a female.

The man had talked to Chelonia the entire time she was in the canoe and while he made measurements and attached the transmitter. He assured her that he was not going to hurt her and that she should be proud to contribute to the body of scientific knowledge. This man was not a commercial turtle trapper but, luckily for Chelonia, was a professional wildlife biologist. Because of the uniqueness of Canaan Valley, this professor from West Virginia University had been studying wildlife in the Valley for over twenty-five years.

The biologist first became aware of the snapping turtles in Canaan Valley while conducting helicopter surveys for waterfowl. During flights, large turtles were frequently spotted in many of the beaver ponds, and he realized these large reptiles were the most prominent predator in the Valley's wetlands. His first attempt to capture snapping turtles involved large hoop nets, with funnel-like openings. Although this style is commonly used in turtle studies, it became apparent that hoop-nets were nearly impossible for one person to manage.

With the assistance of his teen-age son, he had set a large hoop net in a beaver pond on Sand Run one evening in May,

1985. At the beaver pond the next morning, they were greeted by a large snapping turtle entangled in the net. After dragging the net ashore, they proceeded to remove the turtle. But the chore was more difficult than they had anticipated. The net had looped around each of the turtle's legs, around its tail, and most ominously around its head. While the boy held the turtle, the biologist meticulously separated net from animal. As a youngster he had captured smaller turtles, and had never been bitten by one. He had no desire for this thirty-pound mini-beast to clamp its jaws on his fingers. One hour later, the anxious turtle was removed from the net. Blood oozed from two deep, turtle-claw gashes on the boy's arm, but with teen-age toughness he proclaimed the injury to be nothing to worry about. The biologist weighed, measured, and attached a numbered tag to the turtle's shell before returning it to the beaver pond.

Thus began his study of snapping turtles in Canaan Valley. During the next fifteen years he would conduct a detailed study, possibly the most extensive, in-depth study of snapping turtles to be completed in the United States. By 1995, the professor had trapped over ninety turtles and attached transmitters to thirty-five of them. Because snapping turtles were at the top of the food chain in streams and rivers and wetlands throughout the northeastern United States, they were excellent indicators of the health of wetland ecosystems. Their movements, habitat preferences, and hibernation behavior were not fully understood. Thus, the professor had initiated his turtle study to expand the base of scientific knowledge regarding this fascinating reptile.

Activating the receiver, the biologist adjusted it to the 150.200 MHz frequency that identified the particular transmitter attached to Chelonia's shell. A steady, twenty-eight beeps per minute indicated that the transmitter was functioning properly and would enable the biologist to locate the turtle regardless of where she might move. He carefully lifted Chelonia, almost tenderly carried her to the water's edge, and lowered her into the shallow water. She remained motionless for nearly four minutes, then deliberately swam out to deeper water and disappeared from sight. Although she was not visible from shore, the directional antenna attached to the receiver indicated to the biologist exactly where the turtle was swimming. Chelonia thus began her relationship with the wildlife biologist and in so doing entered the segment of her life that would expand scientific knowledge about snapping turtles throughout the Appalachian Mountains.

Chelonia swam across the lake to her favorite daytime resting site and spent the remainder of that day under submerged alder roots. That night she continued her normal activities, unaware that the transmitter was attached to her shell. It weighed only ten ounces, less than one percent of the weight of the large turtle, and was so small that it did not restrict her movements or modify her behavior.

The biologist had transmitters attached to seven other turtles in Sand Run Lake and located all the turtles at least once a week throughout the rest of that summer. During daylight hours the turtles were usually stationary in their daytime retreat, and it was a simple matter to locate them and record their coordinates on maps. At night, when the turtles were active, the biologist was careful not to disturb them and paddled some distance behind as they searched the shallows for food.

The wildlife biologist believed that he had the best job in the world. He was paid (although not much) to do things that other less fortunate souls would, and did, willingly pay to experience. He conducted surveys from helicopters, counting eagles and waterfowl and deer. He conducted bird surveys and counted hawks and woodcock and snipe along with hundreds of kinds of songbirds. He surveyed the endangered West Virginia northern flying squirrel through the use of live traps and nest boxes. He floated by canoe through the Valley on the Blackwater River to count wood duck broods and beaver and herons. But the most rewarding of all activities involved the fascinating snapping turtles. Few biologists had the opportunity to hold a living animal in their hands: to attaçh a transmitter and learn about the animal's daily and seasonal behavior by monitoring its activities, to share (although quite remotely) their problems and their achievements, their births and their deaths. And to experience all of these in Canaan Valley, one of the most fascinating ecosystems in the central Appalachians, was the ultimate reward.

The biologist was constantly reminded of Thoreau's statement in *Walden:* "We need the tonic of wildness—to wade sometimes in marshes where the bittern and the meadow-hen lurk, and hear the booming of the snipe; to smell the whispering sedge where only some wilder and more solitary fowl builds her nest, and the mink crawls with its belly close to the ground." Although it is debatable whether all humans truly need a tonic of wildness, the biologist believed strongly that his life would have been incomplete without wild places and wild animals. Canaan Valley, and neighboring Dolly Sods, offered more wild places and more wild animals than did any other location in West Virginia.

CHAPTER EIGHTEEN

1996-1999: THE WILDLIFE BIOLOGIST

Hibernation was usually an uneventful period in the life of snapping turtles. A few individuals hibernating in a beaver dam had their winter rest disrupted when a flood washed away the dam, as was the case with Chelonia's grandmother. During hibernation, smaller turtles were at much greater peril than were adults. Hungry predators, especially mink and river otter, occasionally located hibernating turtles and dragged them out to obtain an easy meal. While small turtles, especially those at age one to two years, provided little resistance, larger turtles were seldom in danger while hibernating.

The hibernaculum was typically chosen for its capacity to protect against predators, and was usually a large log or the roots of a tree or shrub. Although not fully conscious, hibernating turtles respond when disturbed. A predator wishing to dine on snapping turtle must first escape the jaws and then pull the turtle out from under the carefully chosen, protective shelter. Because of the low water temperatures, usually thirty-four degrees, the claws and jaws of a hibernating snapping turtle lose much of their effectiveness. However, they are still able to dig their claws into the ground and bite with their jaws. The combination of turtle's size, weight, ability to anchor itself in mud, and the potential for a mortal bite all but prevented predators from risking the outcomes.

Mink were common throughout Sand Run, but rarely found hibernating snapping turtles. Their primary prey during winter were muskrats, which they pursued through the water or in their dens and lodges. Although mink rarely exceeded three pounds in weight, they were quite capable of killing muskrats that weighed up to four pounds. The gnawing incisors of a plant-eating herbivore such as a muskrat, were never a match for the killing canines of a carnivore. River otters, in contrast, were a distinct threat to hibernating snapping turtles. Those large carnivores weighed up to twenty-five pounds and had the strength, instincts, and weapons to dig out and kill even larger snapping turtles during winter months. Fortunately for Chelonia and all other snapping turtles living in Canaan Valley, there were few river otter in the Valley. They had been common there during the 1800s, but none existed immediately following the logging and fires. The

WVDNR had reintroduced river otter into many river systems in West Virginia during the 1980s, but none were released into Canaan Valley. Only an occasional otter visited the waterways of Canaan Valley during their wide-ranging explorations following reintroduction.

While hibernating, Chelonia had been detected by a hunting mink several times, but the mink had always moved on in its search for an easy meal. One day in early March, while Chelonia was still in her hibernaculum, she vaguely sensed the presence of something foreign in the water nearby. She felt movement along the edge of her shell and then light contact against her nose. Instinctively she opened her jaws and snapped at the object. It was not the feet of a mink or a river otter or any other potential predator, but the fingers of a human.

The wildlife biologist was conducting his monthly inventory of turtles equipped with transmitters and for which he knew the exact hibernaculum of each individual. Those locations were marked with plastic flagging as soon as the turtles entered hibernation in the fall. The biologist returned to each site monthly to ascertain that the transmitter was still sending out signals and the turtle was still at the site. On that fateful day in March 1998, the first four hibernating turtles he located had not moved since his February field-visit. But when he came to Chelonia's hibernaculum the receiver detected no signals from her transmitter. Since each transmitter operated at a different frequency, it was easy to identify specific turtles. Although a turtle had never left hibernation so early in the year, he pointed the antennae in all directions to determine whether Chelonia had possibly left her hibernaculum and moved into the lake. But the receiver detected no signals on her frequency. While a calamitous event was possible, the most likely explanation was that the batteries had gone dead, and the transmitter was not emitting signals. The reputable and curious scientist would never assume that the battery was dead; he needed proof.

In December he had probed with a wooden dowel and thought he knew the precise spot where Chelonia was resting. She was back under a large hemlock log, about ten inches below the water surface. He probed once again during the March visit, but was not confident he was making contact with the turtle's shell. Like most of his fellow biologists, (and most humans) this biologist had made a few bad decisions in his life, but to his good fortune, none had been serious. The decision he made that day was not a good one. One key characteristic of a good biologist is having above-average curiosity. Curiosity, however, had killed not only cats, but also a few good biologists.

The thermometer read twenty-three degrees when he left the cabin earlier that morning and the wind was blowing hard out of the northwest, creating a dangerous wind-chill factor near zero. A winter storm warning had been issued by the weather service; dropping temperatures and three to five inches of snow were inevitable by nightfall. Six inches of snow already covered the ground as he and Ruffee, his young Brittany spaniel, moved a half-mile above Sand Run Lake. Placing the receiver apparatus on the ground, he removed his down parka and the glove from his right hand. Then he pulled the sleeves of his wool shirt and his insulated sweatshirt up above his elbow. Kneeling down he cautiously reached his right hand beneath the spruce log. He knew he could easily distinguish the front of the turtle's shell from the back, because of the pointed keel-like projections on the top and sides of the turtle's shell. Although the water was uncomfortably cold, his fingers quickly verified his quarry as the top of a turtle's shell. Did the shell belong to Chelonia? Or did another turtle share her hibernaculum? Now all he had to do was slide his fingers around the shell to determine if there was a transmitter present. It would take no longer than thirty seconds to document her presence. He could then withdraw his quickly numbing arm from the water and replace his gloves and parka.

The biologist knew that snapping turtles often hibernated in small groups, with two or three or even four individuals at the same site. On one occasion, two of his turtles with transmitters had spent the winter within two feet of one another. That March day he did not suspect that there was a second turtle hibernating under the hemlock log with Chelonia. As his hand moved around the edge of the turtle he quickly reached the tail and detected no transmitter. Could the turtle have lost the transmitter? It was highly unlikely.

He had started to pull his hand out of the bone-chilling water, when something very sharp clamped around his fingers. He could feel it slice through the skin and then stop when it reached bone. Sheer numbness dulled the excruciating pain and the icy water slowed the blood flow. If his hand had not been so numb he would have probably screamed with pain and jerked his hand backward; and most likely left two fingers in the turtle's jaws. He felt utterly helpless as he watched the blood from his fingers curl up through the water, feeling only the slightest pain. The biologist realized that his fingers were held firmly in a turtle's jaws, nevertheless he attempted to pull his hand gently back. It became obvious, however, that the turtle tightened its grip when he pulled, and he quickly stopped all movement.

The biologist did not panic and scream for help, for it was to no avail. He was certain there was no one to hear him yelling, and he wondered what could be accomplished if help did arrive. It occurred to him that if he remained anchored at that site, he would have a tough time surviving the night.

In a quandary, he tried to calm himself and reason logically. His first thought was to get out his knife. Being right-handed he always carried his knife in his right-hand pocket, but his right hand was held under a hemlock log by a forty-pound snapping turtle. It quickly became apparent one cannot reach into a right-hand pocket with a left hand, while kneeling. There was only one solution; he unbuckled his belt and lowered his trousers to his knees and twisted them around so that he could pull out the knife. Replacing the trousers above his hips, he felt lucky to have put on insulated underwear that morning. But no sooner had he solved one problem then he faced another. How does one perform the impossible task of opening a penknife with one hand? With his teeth, he had removed the glove from his left hand in order to grasp the penknife and that hand was becoming uncomfortably cold. Awkwardly he held the knife in his teeth while his thumb, numb with cold, managed to pull out the four-inch blade.

The knife was now ready to operate. But what was he going to do with it? The years of working with snapping turtles had led to a deep respect for this seldom-appreciated animal. He was probably one of a select few persons who actually liked snapping turtles. He concluded that he was probably not in mortal danger, but serious injury was almost certain for him or the turtle. Now that he had a knife he had two choices: cut off his fingers or hack off the innocent turtle's head. Although the turtle was in a state of torpor it would respond to stimuli, especially a knife slicing into its neck. The biologist reasoned that as soon as the turtle felt the knife against its neck it would react immediately by clamping its jaws even tighter. Truth told, he really did not want to cause the death of this fascinating creature.

Chelonia made no attempt to tighten her grip on the fingers that were seeping blood into her throat. The warm, salty taste of the biologist's blood did not trigger her appetite because her body temperature was only thirty-four degrees, the same as the water. Although the temperature of the biologist's fingers were not thirty-four degrees they were below his normal body temperature and pain from the turtle's grip was minimal. However, the penetrating cold in his forearm and left hand was becoming quite painful.

The biologist lost track of time and could not tell how long he knelt there on the ground, but knew that he had to take some action to prevent a major disaster. He decided that he could cut off his two fingers with little pain because they were nearly totally numb. Thoughts flashed through his consciousness; possibilities had to be entertained, outcomes weighed. Although he was a wildlife biologist who had devoted his entire life to studying wildlife, his favorite pastime was bird hunting with his Brittany spaniel. There were only a few things he enjoyed more than spending a crisp fall day rambling through the aspen thickets of Canaan Valley. If Ruffee made a solid point and he was lucky enough to down a woodcock it was a bonus to a wonderful outing. If they were lucky enough to bag a ruffed grouse it was a pluperfect day.

He concluded that he did not want to lose his shooting finger. He was too old to learn to shoot left-handed and could not learn to shoot with his fourth or fifth finger. He finally decided that he would not cut off his fingers or the head of the turtle.

As a last resort he would jerk his hand back out of the water as suddenly as possible. He might lose all the flesh from his two fingers but the bone should remain attached. He argued to himself that the worst that could happen was the loss of the end digit on his shooting finger.

Before he risked the jerk-and-tear measure, he would make one last effort. In his weary state, he recalled that his grandmother once told him that snapping turtles would not let go until it thundered. However, the odds of thunder in Canaan Valley that March day were pretty slim. Then he remembered a hands-on demonstration he had used during several of his field trips. A captured frog can be quickly put into a trance by gently rubbing its belly. In several demonstrations, he had gently rubbed the belly of a snapping turtle while it was resting on its back on top of a large bucket. The turtles had responded by relaxing their neck and their legs. Would it work with the turtle that was clamped onto his two fingers? Placing the pocket knife back into his left pocket he carefully reached his numbing left hand into the icy water, under the turtle, and began rubbing his fingers along her belly. Possibly the cold had numbed his brain as well as other body parts, because in hindsight, he thought that was not a very wise decision. He realized that a second turtle could have clamped onto his left hand and his troubles would have been amplified beyond resolve.

The biologist was fortunate that day as there were indeed

two turtles under the hemlock log; but his left hand did not come close to the second turtle's jaws. He rubbed and scraped his fingernails on the turtle's belly for what seemed like ten or fifteen minutes, but which was probably much less. Was the grip on his fingers relaxing slightly, or was it wishful thinking? He decided to wait one more minute, then he would attempt to forcibly jerk his fingers out of the turtle's mouth, and accept the outcome. He told himself again that the worst thing that could happen would be the loss of the ends of his two fingers.

Although Chelonia subconsciously realized that the foreign object was still in her mouth, it was motionless and unresisting so she felt no reflexive urge to clamp down. Actually, she attempted to dispel it from her mouth. Her attention was directed toward the strange, but pleasant contact on the underside of her shell. As she focused on the sensation underneath, she began to relax, and her jaws opened slightly. Suddenly there was nothing in her mouth and no further movements on the underside of her shell; and she returned to her undisturbed torpor.

The wildlife biologist felt a mixture of relief, thanksgiving, and freedom as he tried to wipe his hands dry. With much effort he clumsily fastened his trousers and put on his parka. He was not able to put on his gloves, as the air temperature was far lower than that of the moving water. All he could do was put his hands under his armpits inside his wool shirt. His brave spaniel companion, meanwhile, had conducted an extensive search for meadow voles, unconcerned for her master's plight.

Regaining some minimal feeling in his hands, the biologist awkwardly retrieved his antenna and receiver, called his Brittany, and the two retreated to the warm protection of their cabin. They reached the safety of the dwelling just as the leading edge of the snowstorm hit. He awkwardly applied bandages and tape to the injured fingers and decided that a hospital visit was not warranted until the next day. The fingers were throbbing painfully so he was unsure about the safety of driving over the mountains during a winter storm. Throwing some logs into the wood stove, he swallowed two aspirin, fed Ruffee, and brewed a cup of tea. The biologist wondered if anyone would believe his story; moreover, he questioned whether he should reveal to anyone his lackadaisical disregard for safety in checking on a hibernating turtle.

CHAPTER NINETEEN

2000-2002
HUMANS AND DEVELOPMENT

After leaving her hibernaculum and moving down the small stream that fed into Sand Run Lake, Chelonia headed for the shallow muddy shoreline, which warmed more quickly than the main waters of the lake. She spent several sunny days in these shallows, along with most other resident turtles, and slowly her body temperature began to rise. On one April morning as Chelonia rested half asleep, a canoe slowly cruised the shoreline. The wildlife biologist smoothly dipped his paddle into the water, attempting to move soundlessly with no sudden movements. He was in search of turtles. His experience had shown that they rested in the shallows during spring and, with care, he could get as close as five or six feet before they spotted his canoe and submerged out of sight.

Chelonia spotted the canoe at fifteen feet, and she eased away from the shoreline. The biologist spotted her as she started swimming and immediately propelled the canoe toward her. Keeping the canoe paddle on the opposite side of the canoe from the turtle, he closed the distance between him and Chelonia. Most turtles would have dived and dug into the bottom mud to escape detection. Chelonia, however, was seriously handicapped by the blindness in her right eye. Fortunately the biologist happened to be on her right side, and he could see the transmitter on the rear of her shell. He wanted desperately to capture her. A triangle of orange plastic flagging attached to the transmitter immediately identified her as the turtle that had bitten his fingers the previous winter. Her transmitter was no longer sending out signals, and he wanted to replace it with a new one.

Picking up a long-handled net with a hoop nearly two feet in diameter, he slipped it into the water and maneuvered it beneath the large turtle. When in place, he quickly lifted up on the handle and the turtle slid neatly into the bottom of the net. Holding the netted reptile, the biologist moved into the center of the canoe, knelt on the bottom, and struggled to lift the massive turtle's dead weight out of the water. After a few minutes of maneuvering and nearly tipping the canoe, Chelonia was resting motionless in the front of the canoe.

Paddling to the shore, he carefully lifted Chelonia out of the canoe, dropped the net away, and placed her gently upside down on a large plastic bucket. Using pliers and screwdriver he easily removed the brass bolts that held the original transmitter in place. He exchanged the old one with a fresh transmitter from his toolbox and quickly attached it to the turtle with a new set of brass bolts and nuts. After weighing and measuring the turtle he carefully carried her to the lake and released her as he had done six years before. The battery-life of the transmitters ranged from two to four years, although another turtle's set of batteries had lasted seven years. With luck this new transmitter would yield at least three more year's data on Chelonia.

He had learned much about her during the four years her batteries emitted signals, but a biologist could never have too much data. So far, he knew she selected the same log for her hibernaculum, year after year, and he could pinpoint her favorite spots in the lake to feed and to rest. He had documented that she remained in the upper end of the lake during most of the summer, but on occasion wandered into the beaver pond located upstream from the lake. He also determined that she might be the oldest turtle he had ever captured. While biologists had no definitive process by which to age turtles accurately, their size and weight were good indicators of their age.

Unbeknown to the biologist, Chelonia was fifty-six years old. She was the oldest living turtle and the oldest living animal—excluding humans—in Canaan Valley. She had found near optimum habitat in Sand Run Lake. Food was plentiful and shelter was more than adequate. She weighed nearly forty-two pounds, she had mated and laid a clutch of eggs each year since she moved into Sand Run Lake, and two of the clutches had escaped predation and produced over seventy hatchling turtles. Although most of the hatchlings had been eaten by predators before they reached one year of age, twelve of her offspring were living in the lake. It appeared that Chelonia would successfully create a new generation of snapping turtles possessing the genes and the instincts that enabled her to survive so long.

Wildlife populations in Sand Run Lake and most of the Valley were more diverse and abundant than they had ever been in the history of Canaan Valley. Natural succession had produced a diversity of habitat types, which in turn had produced a diversity of wildlife. Goose numbers had grown to over five hundred, thanks to the golf course, the man-made lakes, and the beaver ponds scattered throughout the northern end of the Valley. At least three hundred beaver thrived in Canaan and the ponds and beaver meadows they created provided habitat for thousands of other animals. The deer herd had exploded past the five thousand count, in spite of annual harvests exceeding one thousand animals.

With more than one hundred species of birds and forty species of mammals in the Valley, the conglomeration provided an excellent prey base for the resident predators. At least thirty species of medium-to-large predators were present at some time of the year in Canaan Valley, indicating that the Canaan valley ecosystem was relatively healthy.

Raptors were the most visible of all predators. In winter, bald eagles fed on fish while golden eagles scavenged on dead deer or preyed on weak or injured deer. A variety of hawks nested in the Valley, including the kestrel (sparrow hawk), red-tailed, red-shouldered, broad-winged, sharp-shinned, and Coopers. Other raptors, including the osprey, northern harrier (marsh hawk), and rough-legged hawk were winter visitors. Barred owls, great-horned owls, screech owls, and saw-whet owls were all permanent residents nesting in the Valley.

Mammalian predators were not quite so diverse as avian predators, but were all year-round residents. Most common were the raccoons, bobcats, gray foxes, red foxes, mink, fisher, long-tailed weasels, and striped skunks. Black bear numbers had increased to nuisance levels and were a threat to humans. Coyotes had immigrated into the Valley and the abundant numbers of deer, groundhogs, and geese sustained them. Mountain lions were reported each year.

One hundred and twenty adult snapping turtles lived in Sand Run Lake. Like Chelonia, most had wandered up Sand Run, while others wandered cross-country from Yoakum Run and Spruce Island Lake. A few had lived in the upper reaches of Sand Run before the lake was constructed and those eventually made their way downstream to the lake. Some had been born in the lake and never left it.

The habitat within Sand Run Lake was nearly ideal for Chelonia and the other snapping turtles, except for one thing: humans. While the wildlife populations had increased in Canaan Valley so had the human population. Although no one hunted turtles in Sand Run Lake humans were nevertheless a threat. Fishing was common in the lake, especially during summer months. Some fishermen used live bait, and worms and minnows were tempting to turtles just as they were to fish. But humans offered direct, as well as indirect, threats to snapping turtles. The earthen dam that created Sand Run Lake was nearly an ideal place for turtles to lay their eggs. Just a short trip from the water to the top of the dam, the soil was loose enough for turtles to easily dig an egg chamber. Grasses grew on the dam, but geese kept them grazed down so that there were many bare sandy sites ideal for a female snapping turtle. Humans often spotted turtles that were laying eggs, but typically they did not disturb the females. However, this was not always the case.

One day in late June, the wildlife biologist was tracking turtles equipped with transmitters and the signals for an adult female were coming from the dam. Expecting that she was nesting, he hurried to find her before she had completed the annual chore. Approaching the end of the dam, he saw what appeared to be a large turtle lying in the grass. He approached cautiously so as not to frighten the female, but as he got closer he saw that it was dead. The transmitter was still sending out signals, but someone had beaten the turtle with a heavy club until she died. Her shell was cracked open and over twenty white eggs could be seen inside her body cavity. Apparently she had not yet started to lay eggs when she was discovered, and destroyed. The transmitter was quite visible on the rear of the turtle's shell, and the commission of such a mean-spirited act appalled the biologist. He gently carried the turtle to his canoe and then back to his cabin, where he recorded all the pertinent measurements. It saddened him to lose one of his research turtles, but it saddened him even more to think that any human would commit such a heinous act.

Although the plant and animal communities of Canaan Valley had shown remarkable recovery in the short time since logging, there were other threats to the continued recovery of these natural communities. The northern end of the Valley remained undeveloped and the threat of the Davis Power Project had apparently ended. The U. S. Court of Appeals ruled that a Clean Water Act permit was required for the power project. But, because the project would have inundated over six thousand acres of wetlands, the Power Company had been denied a permit. Following several legal appeals, the U.S. Supreme Court announced in 1988 that it would not review the lower-court decision. Thus, the Supreme Court ruling doomed the Davis Power Project.

But what would happen to the northern end of the Valley, the twenty thousand acres that were owned by two large corporations? Would it be developed or preserved? The U.S. Fish and Wildlife Service had approved the establishment of the Canaan Valley National Wildlife Refuge in 1979, but by the year 2000 they had managed to purchase only a few hundred acres in the southern end of the Valley. Those small parcels were scattered among farms and housing developments and businesses and although they were significant acquisitions, without the twenty thousand acres in the northern end, the refuge could not protect, or represent, the unique Canaan Valley ecosystem.

Development had increased during the 1980s, and in addition to destroying wildlife habitat through construction of homes and businesses, there was a never-ending demand placed on the water resources. Houses and restaurants, lodges and businesses, and ski slopes and golf courses required great amounts of water. In return they created huge amounts of waste that were returned to the streams and water table. The streams, wetlands, and water table would be seriously impacted if development continued. And of course, all the plants and animals that depended upon plentiful amounts of clean water would also be impacted.

APS ownership of vast acreage in Canaan Valley was accompanied by constant public debate over its proposed power project and the associated seven thousand-acre lake. Although environmental groups frequently portrayed the Power Company as the villain, it actually may have been the unwitting guardian of the Valley and its wetlands, providing long-term protection against many types of development. So long as the Power Company owned those lands situated below 3,280 feet elevation (and this included all wetlands), along with most of the surrounding mountainsides in the northern two-thirds of the Valley, development could not occur. According to federal law, lands owned by public utilities could be used, or held, solely for purposes of power production, and could not be developed for any other purposes. Had the northern end of Canaan Valley not been purchased by the Power Company in 1923, individuals and/or companies would likely have drained and flooded many of the Valley's valuable wetlands. In addition, numerous vacation homes and associated recreational developments would have been constructed in and around wetlands, and on the mountainsides surrounding wetlands. Not until 1970 was the value of wetlands officially recognized, and only then did they receive any protection by state or federal governments. To date, equally valuable uplands have received no similar protection.

The Fourth of July weekend 2001 brought the usual number of fishermen to Sand Run Lake and Chelonia retreated to the dense protective cover of the downed trees along the eastern shoreline of the lake. The unusually large number of canoes disturbed Chelonia and she did not begin feeding until total darkness had settled over the Valley. Two weeks later, after the Independence Day crowd had returned home, wildlife activities returned to normal. Only a few canoes ventured onto the lake and most of those were during the weekend. Geese were molting and unable to fly. Female wood ducks and mallards led their broods through the dense stands of cattails and sedges where invertebrates were abundant. The beaver kits from the two families residing in Sand Run Lake were large enough to venture outside the lodge, and they were learning where to find the tender pondweeds.

Chelonia was searching through the flooded alder for the large crayfish that crawled up onto the woody stems after nightfall. Largemouth bass also relished crayfish, and as a result the flooded alder was a favorite fishing site for the serious anglers that visited the lake. Chelonia pushed her way through the stems and branches and was unconcerned when her shell temporarily became entangled in an alder branch. With only a slight amount of pulling she broke free and continued her search. With her powerful legs and curved claws Chelonia was always able to move through or under or around any obstacle she encountered. If necessary she could dig under; or she could simply force her way through. Occasionally a turtle became permanently entrapped, but it was always a freak accident when that occurred. Chelonia had encountered only one turtle whose life ended because of such an accident.

It was probably true that no natural obstacle could endanger

Chelonia. There were, however, unnatural obstacles and dangers in Sand Run Lake. Later that night Chelonia's movements were once again halted. She pushed and pulled. She swam down toward the bottom and up toward the surface. But something was holding her. She struggled wildly, but to no avail. Although she did not panic, as would most air-breathing animals, she was aware of the danger facing her. If water temperatures had been lower and her normal body processes had slowed significantly she could have remained under water for several hours, or even days. But water temperatures were above seventy-five degrees and there was little available oxygen in the water. She could possibly remain under water for two hours, but not much longer.

Chelonia was tangled in nylon fishing line. Two weeks earlier a fisherman had hooked a large bass that darted into the submerged alder to escape. Although the bass could not pull lose, it managed to wrap the line around an alder branch. The fisherman pulled and tugged, but his efforts were fruitless and his line broke. The bass managed to pull loose later that night, but the hook and nearly twenty feet of line remained submerged in the water. In what could only be labeled a freak accident, the hook had caught the edge of Chelonia's shell. As she attempted to pull lose, the line twisted around her front leg and then around the pointed keels at the rear of her shell. The ten-pound line should have slid off her leg and past her shell but instead it tightened. Nylon fishing line has the uncanny ability to twist into loops and then into knots that are nearly impossible for a fishermen to untangle. Chelonia could have broken the line if it had been attached firmly to a solid object. But the alder stem was somewhat flexible and it moved as she pulled against it. The fishing line held her about twelve inches below the surface of the water. But twelve inches or twelve feet, it did not matter. She could not extend her nostrils above the water to reach the life-giving air. Chelonia was in serious jeopardy.

The wildlife biologist was in his canoe that night following two turtles equipped with transmitters to learn more about their nighttime feeding forays around the lake. One turtle had spent the day in a large cove along the western shore, then as dusk arrived it left the cove and swam toward the dam. It moved into and out of two coves, before swimming back toward the upper end of the lake. The biologist followed another turtle for nearly twenty minutes then quickly checked the locations of five other turtles that he had equipped with transmitters. He located Chelonia in the flooded alder and was somewhat surprised that her signals were coming from nearly the same place where he had located her earlier in the evening. The alder was not one of her favorite resting places, but he had found her resting in similar sites on other occasions. It was late and he was tired; he would return the next morning.

Chelonia struggled for a short time, but as her oxygen supply was depleted she ceased all movements. She entered a state of torpor, her body processes slowed drastically, and she lost consciousness. The next morning the biologist loaded his receiver and antennae into his canoe and headed for the spot where he had picked up Chelonia's signals the previous night. Again he was surprised to find that the signal seemed to come from the same site near the center of the flooded alder. Moving his canoe so that he did not block the rays from the morning sun, he flipped down his Raybans and peered into the water. He saw something glistening and when he put his face closer to the water he realized it was one of his transmitters. It must be the one he had attached to Chelonia, but he could not imagine why she was not moving. He carefully touched the turtle's shell with the end of his canoe paddle and immediately realized that something was wrong. Reaching his arm into the water he found that he could not pull her up to the surface. His fingers detected the fishing line and he instantly knew what had happened. As he pulled the knife from his pocket he remembered the last time he had pulled out a knife in the presence of this same turtle. This time he did not have to worry about injuring the large female turtle, or her injuring him. She was dead!

The biologist sat reflecting quietly in the canoe for nearly an hour. After gently laying the turtle on the bottom of the canoe, he removed the fishing line from around her shell. He examined the shortened tail and wondered what accident had caused her to lose nearly four inches of the tip. He counted the large leeches that were still attached to the underside of her legs and neck. He opened her mouth and felt the sharp jaws that had clamped onto his two fingers that cold March day. He carefully examined all the scars on her shell and the sunken right eye and the missing claws on her hind foot and wondered about their origin. He tried to imagine the life of an animal that old. What interesting sights had she seen? What experiences had she survived? How many more years would she have lived if the accident had not occurred? But most of all he wondered if he could have saved her life had he taken a few minutes to shine his flashlight down into the water the previous night. He would always wonder, but would never know.

EPILOGUE

On February 14, 2002, Senator Robert C. Byrd announced that Allegheny Energy (formerly APS) had agreed to sell twelve thousand acres of land to the U. S. Fish and Wildlife Service. The land, situated in the northern end of the Valley, significantly expanded the Canaan Valley National Wildlife Refuge.

The majority of the Valley's wetlands, with the exception of a portion of the Little Blackwater drainage in the northeastern end, were finally protected. Protection provided by Canaan Valley National Wildlife Refuge, Canaan Valley State Park, and existing wetland laws will provide assurance that no development occurs within the Valley's wetlands. Beaver ponds and sphagnum bogs, along with streams and tributaries, will continue to provide adequate habitat for snapping turtles, and all wetland wildlife, for many decades to come.

The Blackwater 100 was discontinued in 1994. In 1995, Allegheny Power System posted signs throughout all its lands in the Valley, restricting off-road vehicles to certain roads. Although total enforcement was impossible, ATV impacts to the wetlands and associated plant and animal communities were reduced.

But threats to the wetlands and their wildlife still exist. A portion of the upland habitats surrounding the wetlands is still owned by Allegheny Energy and Western Pocahontas Properties. If the course of history is any determinant, development of their lands is imminent. The only unknown is the nature and degree of development. Canaan Valley is within one day's drive of more than one-third of the Nation's population. Corridor H, a controlled-access, four-lane highway, is planned to pass within one mile of the northern end of the Valley, and upon completion will make the Valley even more accessible to visitors.

There will always be snapping turtles in Canaan Valley, along with beaver and woodcock and green frogs. But will the wildness that characterized the northern two-thirds of Canaan Valley be lost to commercial development? Such a misfortune will be prevented only when the twenty thousand acres comprising a remnant of the great wilderness of the 1800s are so governed that the impacts of humans are minimal.

Much of the Canaan Valley story is history, but one major chapter—that involving human impacts—lies in the future and is yet to be written.

In his book, *Sand County Almanac*, Aldo Leopold maintains that like rainbows and sunsets and shooting stars, wild things were taken for granted, until progress began to do away with them. But he asks whether a higher standard of living is worth its cost in wild things and wild and natural places. For those of us in the minority, the opportunity to see mink and muskrats and wood ducks is more important than television, and the chance to find a clump of skunk cabbage along a secluded woodland stream or a stand of cotton grass scattered throughout a boggy marsh is a right we do not want to lose.

CHRONOLOGY OF MAJOR EVENTS IN HISTORY OF CANAAN VALLEY

1746 - First non-Indian visitors entered Canaan Valley: surveying party engaged in locating boundaries for the Lord Fairfax Northern Neck proprietary.

1748 - George Harness, a fur trader, proclaimed, "Behold the land of Canaan" as he looked down into the Valley from Cabin Mountain.

1779 - Heinrich Fanchler became the Valley's first settler. He survived only one winter in the Valley before moving to the present-day site of Hendricks.

1864 - First farm developed in the Valley.

1888 - First commercial logging in the Valley.

1915 - Railroads built into Valley to haul out timber.

1920 - Land purchased for Monongahela National Forest, primarily in the western and southeastern ends of the Valley.

1922 - Logging of virgin forests completed in Canaan Valley.

1923 - West Virginia Power and Transmission Company purchased 13,230 acres from Babcock Lumber and Boom Company for construction of a hydroelectric power plant.

1925 - Railroads into Valley were abandoned; rails removed.

1926 - West Virginia Conservation Commission (now WVDNR) released white-tailed deer in the Valley.

1932 - Current state road (State Route 32) built through the Valley from Davis to Harman.

1936 - West Virginia Conservation Commission stocked beaver in the Valley.

1938 - Electricity brought into the Valley.

1942 - Gas wells drilled in the Valley.

1954 - Cauliflower and broccoli raised commercially in the Valley.

1956 - Washington Ski Club opened first downhill ski slopes in Valley.

1957 - First land obtained for Canaan Valley State Park.

1959 - West Virginia Central and Pittsburgh Railway Co. (later known as Western Maryland Railroad and eventually Western Pocahontas Properties) purchased 2,100 acres in northern end of Valley.

1963 - WVDNR stocked largemouth bass in the Valley.

1969 - WVDNR released Canada geese in the Valley

1969 - WVDNR released fisher in the Valley.

1970 - Allegheny Power applied for a permit to construct a hydroelectric project in Canaan Valley.

1971 - Canaan Valley State Park ski resort opened.

1972 - Canaan Valley State Park golf course opened.

1973 - Allegheny Properties purchased three thousand acres for development: later known as Timberline Vacation Home Development.

1975 - First Blackwater 100 (off-road vehicle race).

1977 - Canaan Valley State Park lodge opened.

1977 - The Federal Power Commission issued a license to Allegheny Power to construct the Davis Power Project, a pumped storage hydroelectric project. This power project would have inundated approximately six thousand acres of wetlands and two thousand acres of terrestrial habitat.

1978 - Following public hearings, the Davis Power Project was denied a "Clean Water Act Permit" by the U. S. Army Corps of Engineers, citing the project's potentially extensive adverse impacts on wetlands.

1979 - The U. S. Fish and Wildlife Service approved the establishment of the Canaan Valley National Wildlife Refuge.

1981 - Timberline Ski Resort opened (formerly Allegheny Properties).

1988 - In response to Allegheny Power's appeal to the U. S. Supreme Court, that body elected not to review a U. S. Court of Appeals decision that a Clean Water Act permit was required for the Davis Power Project. That decision doomed the Davis Power Project.

1994 - Blackwater 100 discontinued.

1994 - First land purchased by the U.S.F.W.S. for Canaan Valley National Wildlife Refuge.

2002 - Allegheny Power sold twelve thousand acres of their 1923 purchase to U.S.F.W.S. for addition to Canaan Valley National Wildlife Refuge.

ABOUT THE AUTHOR

Dr. Michael is a native West Virginian. He was born on Plum Run, near Mannington and Farmington, attended elementary school at Shinnston, and graduated from Magnolia High School in New Martinsville. He received a B.S. in Biology from Marietta College and M.S. and Ph.D. degrees in Wildlife Ecology from Texas A&M University. After teaching six years at Stephen F. Austin State University in Nacogdoches, Texas, Dr. Michael returned to his beloved state and taught at West Virginia University from 1970 through 1997. Following retirement from West Virginia University, he was awarded the title of Professor Emeritus in 1998. His forty-year-career as a wildlife biologist has produced more than one hundred publications, both scientific and popular. During that time he became a part-time resident of Canaan Valley, conducted research, directed wildlife surveys, hunted for grouse and woodcock, fished for bass and trout, dug ramps, picked blueberries, skied cross-country, canoed the Blackwater River, conducted numerous field trips, and hiked hundreds of miles. He directed the wildlife studies for the Davis Power Project, studied snapping turtles, and conducted surveys for the endangered West Virginia northern flying squirrel. He continues to be an active researcher and outdoorsman.